Dirty Bertie

HEAPS of HAVOC

DAVID ROBERTS WRITTEN BY ALAN MACDONALD

Collect all the Dirty Bertie books!

Contents

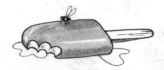

STRIPES PUBLISHING
An imprint of the Little Tiger Group
1 The Coda Centre, 189 Munster Road,
London SW6 6AW

A paperback original
First published in Great Britain in 2017

ISBN: 978-1-84715-797-3

Characters created by David Roberts
Text copyright © Alan MacDonald
Smash! 2014 • Rats! 2014 • Jackpot! 2015
Illustrations copyright © David Roberts
Smash! 2014 • Rats! 2014 • Jackpot! 2015

Printed and bound in the UK.

10 9 8 7 6 5 4 3 2 1

Dirty Bertie

SMASH!

For Isabelle, who I met at the Bath Literary Festival – here's another book for your collection ~ D R

For Riley, a dedicated Bertie fan ~ A M

Contents

CHAPTER 1

Bertie and his friends were playing
football in the back garden. As usual,
Bertie was providing the commentary.
"And it's Bertie on the ball," he yelled.
"He goes past Darren – this is brilliant –
he cuts inside … he takes a shot …
he must score! "
THUMP!

The ball whizzed over Eugene and the fence…

SMASH!

Bertie held his head.

"You nutter!" groaned Darren. "What did you do that for?"

They went to the fence and peeped through a crack. At the end of the lawn stood the Nicelys' greenhouse. One of the windows had a gaping hole.

"Yikes! Now look what you've done!" said Eugene.

"Why didn't you stop it?" moaned Bertie.

"It was a mile over the bar – I'm not Superman!" said Eugene.

"Anyway, it wasn't a goal," said Darren.

"It's still 2–1 to me."

"Never mind that!" said Bertie. "What are we going to DO? Mrs Nicely will go raving mad when she sees that window."

Eugene shook his head. "I *told* you we should have gone to the park."

Bertie didn't think his friends grasped the seriousness of the situation. It wasn't any old window they'd broken. The greenhouse was practically new and it was Mrs Nicely's pride and joy. She was always in there planting or potting or whatever people did in greenhouses.

And to make matters worse, Bertie wasn't exactly in Mrs Nicely's good

books. Only last week Whiffer had left
a smelly present on next-door's lawn.
Bertie didn't like to think what would
happen when she saw the broken
window. Her scream would be heard
halfway to Timbuktu. She would be
round in no time to see his parents.
Football in the garden would be banned,
and he'd probably be paying for the
damage for the next six years.

He glanced at the house. No one
seemed to have heard the crash. *No
one can actually prove it was me*, thought
Bertie. Then he remembered – the
football. The moment Mrs Nicely saw
it she'd *know* who was responsible. The
only other neighbour was grumpy Mr
Monk, and Bertie was pretty sure he'd
never kicked a ball in his life!

"We're dead!" groaned Bertie.

"*You're* dead you mean," said Darren.

"What's the difference?" said Bertie. "Our only hope's to get the ball back."

"Good idea," said Eugene. "Off you go then."

"ME?" said Bertie.

"*You* kicked it over!" said Eugene.

"Yes, but we were all playing," argued Bertie. "It could have been any of us."

"It wasn't, it was you," said Darren.

Bertie didn't see why *he* should be
the one to risk his life. Mrs Nicely knew
where he lived. If anything, it made far
more sense for Darren or Eugene to go.

"I know, why don't we toss a coin?"
he suggested.

"No way! I'm not going," said Darren.

Dirty Bertie

"I've heard Mrs Nicely when she shouts."

"Don't look at *me*," said Eugene.
"I wanted to play in the park."

Bertie sighed. He thought friends were meant to help each other out. But it seemed that as soon as you smashed a window with a football, you were on your own.

He peeped through the fence at next-door's garden. Mr Nicely didn't come home till late, but that still left Angela and her mum. To reach the greenhouse Bertie would have to cross the lawn — and he knew for a fact that the Nicelys had a burglar alarm. What if it went off as soon as he set foot on the grass?

CHAPTER 2

While they were thinking what to do, Whiffer appeared. He trotted over to Bertie and licked his hand.

"Not now, Whiffer, I'm busy," sighed Bertie. Then an idea came to him. He was saved! "We'll send Whiffer!"

The other two looked at him blankly.

"Send him where?" said Darren.

"Next door, dumbo! Whiffer can get the ball!"

Darren and Eugene exchanged looks. Some dogs could perform amazing tricks, but this was Whiffer they were talking about.

"You're not serious?" said Darren. "You can't even get him to lie down!"

Bertie had to admit that this was true. Last September his mum had forced him to take Whiffer to training classes. After six weeks of yelling at Whiffer to stay, sit and roll over, Bertie had given up. Whiffer was about as obedient as a Brussels sprout. All the same, Bertie only wanted him to fetch a ball – surely *any* dog could manage that?

Dirty Bertie

Bertie led Whiffer down the garden to where there was a gap in the fence.

"Ball," said Bertie. "Go on, Whiffer, fetch the ball!"

He pointed to the Nicelys' garden. Whiffer jumped up at his hand, thinking it was a game.

Darren sighed. "You're wasting your time! Just get it yourself."

"Yes, and get a move on before anyone comes," said Eugene anxiously.

"He can do it," Bertie insisted. "Watch this."

He looked around and found a stick. "Fetch, Whiffer! Fetch!" he cried, throwing it with all his might. Whiffer gave a bark and raced off after it. A moment later he was back with the stick in his mouth. He dropped it at Bertie's feet and barked excitedly.

"See, I told you!" said Bertie.

"Yeah," said Darren. "If we need any sticks we know who to ask."

"Darren's right," said Eugene. "It's a football. He can't even pick it up."

"Want to bet?" asked Bertie. He led

Dirty Bertie

Whiffer back to the fence and helped him squeeze through the hole. "Good boy, bring the ball," he whispered.

Whiffer ran off and vanished into next-door's bushes.

"It'll never work," said Darren.

"Not a hope," said Eugene.

"You wait," said Bertie. "He's smarter than you think."

There was a rustle in the bushes and a patter of feet. Whiffer came flying through the hole in the fence. He dropped something at Bertie's feet and wagged his tail.

"Fantastic," groaned Darren.

It was another stick.

CHAPTER 3

Bertie was left with no choice – he'd have to sneak next door himself. They'd wasted precious minutes already. At any moment someone might come out and then it would be too late.

"How do I look?" he asked.

"Filthy," said Eugene.

Bertie had mud smeared over his face

so he'd be less easy to spot. It always worked in spy films.

"Keep a look out," he said. "If anyone comes, give the signal."

The other two nodded.

Bertie wriggled through the gap in the fence. Once next door, he crouched in the bushes, his heart beating loudly. There was no sign of the enemy. He could see the greenhouse – but now he had to make it across the lawn.

He crawled forward on his belly, passing a statue of a small fat angel. Halfway across the lawn he froze – someone was coming! A moment later Mrs Nicely appeared with a magazine and a steaming mug of coffee. Bertie looked round in panic. He rolled over and crouched behind the statue – it was the only hiding place. With any luck Mrs Nicely would go back inside.

But instead she came down the steps and settled on a bench. Bertie rested his head against the statue's bottom. Now what? He was trapped! And if Mrs Nicely looked up from her magazine she'd spot the broken window.

Bertie looked back at Darren and Eugene peeping through the fence.

"DO SOMETHING!" he mouthed.

Darren frowned.

"DO SOMETHING! ANYTHING!" Bertie mouthed again.

He tried to think. What would distract Mrs Nicely's attention so he could escape? An earthquake? An alien invasion? What were the chances! Wait – Whiffer! Mrs Nicely flew into a rage whenever he got into her garden.

Bertie tried to signal to his friends. He stuck out his tongue, panting like a dog. The other two stared back.

"What's he doing?" whispered Eugene.

Dirty Bertie

"No idea," said Darren. "Maybe he feels sick."

Bertie scratched his ear and pretended to wag his tail.

"Is he all right?" asked Eugene.

"If you ask me, he's gone bonkers," said Darren.

Bertie might have been stuck there forever but just then Angela appeared. "Mum! Where are the chocolate biscuits?" she called.

Mrs Nicely groaned. "Can't I have five minutes' peace and quiet? Look in the cupboard."

"I did. There aren't any!" grumbled Angela.

Mrs Nicely got to her feet with a sigh and headed for the house. The back door slammed. Bertie didn't wait a second longer. He tore through the bushes and shot back through the hole in the fence.

"Well?" said Darren. "Did you get the football?"

"You've got to be joking," panted Bertie. "I am NEVER doing that again!"

CHAPTER 4

They were dead meat, doomed, done for. Sooner or later Mrs Nicely would notice the broken window and find the football.

"Doo-dee doo-dee doo… !"

A shrill voice floated over the fence. Angela! She was back outside. Perhaps *she* would be able to help. Angela was

in love with Bertie and told everyone
that he was her boyfriend. Normally
Bertie avoided her like a cold bath, but
not today – she was their last hope. He
walked over to the fence.

"Psst! Angela!" he hissed.

"Is that you, Bertie?" asked Angela.

"Of course it's me. Listen, I need your
help. It's very important," said Bertie.

Angela nodded seriously. "Are we
looking for dinosaur footprints?"

"Not this time," said Bertie. "You see
the greenhouse?"

Angela turned and gasped. "Umm!
Someone broke the window!"

"Yes… Never mind that," said Bertie.
"There's a football in there and I need
you to get it, okay?"

Angela frowned. "Is it your football?"

"Yes," said Bertie.

"Actually it's mine," said Darren. "But Bertie booted it over."

"Is that how you broke the window?" asked Angela, wide-eyed.

"Look, never mind about the window," said Bertie. "Just go and find the football. It's *really* important we get it back."

Angela was silent for a while, thinking. "What do *I* get?" she said at last.

"You?"

"Yes, if I get the ball for you, what do I get?"

Bertie rolled his eyes at his friends. By now they should have known that nothing with Angela was ever simple. Luckily they'd been to the sweet shop that morning.

Dirty Bertie

"I'll give you a jelly snake," he said. "It's my last one."

"Where is it?" said Angela. Bertie poked the snake through the crack in the fence. Angela grabbed it and bit off the head.

"What else?" she said, chewing.

"What do you mean, what else? That's my last jelly snake!" grumbled Bertie.

"I know, but now I've eaten it," said Angela.

Bertie ground his teeth. This was robbery. But if they wanted the ball they didn't have any choice. He held out his hand to Darren and

Eugene, and reluctantly they parted with their goodies. Angela accepted two fizzy bootlaces and a half-sucked lollipop.

"*Now* will you get the ball?" said Bertie.

"Okay!" sang Angela, dancing away from them.

A minute later they heard a ball bouncing on the lawn.

"Great," called Bertie. "Hurry up!"

THUD, THUD, THUD! The ball went on bouncing.

"Throw it over!" cried Bertie impatiently. "You promised!"

Angela shook her head. "I promised I'd get it, I didn't say I'd give it back."

She went on bouncing – she'd always wanted her own ball.

Dirty Bertie

Bertie couldn't believe it. They'd been tricked. Cheated out of their sweets — and all for nothing.

"ANGELA!"

The bouncing suddenly stopped. Mrs Nicely had returned. Bertie and his friends ducked down behind the fence to avoid her.

"Angela, where did you get that ball?" she demanded.

Angela said nothing. If she admitted it wasn't hers she'd have to give it back.

Mrs Nicely marched down the lawn. "You know what I think about footballs," she scolded. "Things always get broken. If you don't—" She stopped, catching sight of the smashed window.

Dirty Bertie

"ANGELA!" she screeched.

"But it wasn't me…" said Angela.

"Don't tell lies!" snapped Mrs Nicely. "Give me that ball – and go to your room, right now!"

Angela's lip wobbled. She dropped the ball and fled indoors, wailing all the way. "WAAAAAAH!"

Mrs Nicely picked up the muddy football. Nasty horrible thing! She hurled it over her shoulder and stormed inside.

THUD!

The ball landed over the fence, bouncing twice. Bertie blinked at it, astonished.

"Crumbs! It came back!" he said.

"And we're not in trouble," said Eugene. "She thinks Angela did it!"

Bertie picked up the football and spun it round. "Come on then, let's finish the game," he said. "Next goal's the winner!"

CHAPTER 1

Bertie had just got back from school. As usual on a Friday, Gran had dropped in for tea.

"What's this, Bertie? It was in your pocket," asked Mum.

"Oh yes," said Bertie. "It's a letter from school. I was going to give it to you."

Mum read it out.

"Goodie!" said Gran. "I love bingo! Can we go?"

Mum shook her head. "Not on Saturday, we're taking Suzy to her dance show. But you can go."

"What? By myself?" said Gran.

"Take Bertie, he might like it," suggested Mum.

"ME? Why me?" asked Bertie.

Dirty Bertie

"I'm sure other children will be there," said Mum. "It'll be fun."

"Not if it's at school," said Bertie. It was bad enough having to go all week, without being dragged there on a Saturday night! Anyway, bingo was for grannies. Why didn't school put on something *he'd* enjoy – like mud wrestling? "It'll be boring!" he moaned.

"No it won't," said Gran. "Bingo's dead exciting."

"Only if you're over a hundred," said Bertie gloomily.

"Anyone can play," said Gran. "Everyone has a bingo card and the idea's to collect all the numbers as they're called out. The first one to do it wins!"

Bertie pulled a face. It sounded as exciting as laying the table.

"Can't I just stay at home and watch TV?" he begged.

"Suit yourself," said Gran. "But I won't be sharing my prizes."

Bertie blinked. "Prizes?"

"Of course," said Gran. "You can't have bingo without prizes."

"What sort of prizes?"

Gran shrugged. "I don't know – toys, chocolates, TV sets maybe…"

"TV SETS?" yelled Bertie. They desperately needed a new super-widescreen TV. Their TV was so small you practically needed a magnifying glass to watch it!

"I wouldn't get your hopes up," said Mum. "It's only a school bingo night."

"There's free pizza as well," said Gran. "It says so in the letter."

Dirty Bertie

Free pizza? That settled it. There was no way Bertie was going to miss a night like that!

CHAPTER 2

They were late arriving on Saturday,
mainly because it took Gran about six
hours to get ready. The school hall was
crowded with people by the time they
got there. Tables and chairs were set
out to face a platform at the front. To
Bertie's dismay all of the seats seemed
to be taken. He spotted Darren and

Dirty Bertie

Eugene but they were with their families.

"What about that table? They've got seats," said Gran, pointing.

Bertie groaned. "No way! I'm not sitting next to Know-All Nick!"

"You don't have to talk to him," said Gran. "Anyway, there's nowhere else."

Bertie trailed after her and flopped into the seat beside his old enemy. It looked like Nick had brought his gran too. She was wearing a sparkly gold dress and her hair was piled on her head like whipped cream. Bertie thought she looked as if she was having dinner with the Queen.

"Not sitting with your friends?" sneered Nick.

"No, I'm stuck with you, worst luck," sighed Bertie.

Dirty Bertie

Nick held his nose. "Pooh! You could have had a bath," he sniffed.

"You could have stayed at home," answered Bertie, turning his back.

Across the table the two grannies were getting to know each other.

"So nice to meet you," said Nick's grandma. "I'm Julia."

"I'm Dotty," said Gran. "Have you played bingo before?"

"Oh, I hardly think so," sniffed Julia.

"Me and Sherry go every Wednesday," said Gran.

"That must be nice for you," said Julia snootily.

Bertie rolled his eyes. He could tell they were in for a long evening.

Dirty Bertie

Miss Boot, their Bingo Caller for the
night, sat down on the stage. Her job
was to call out the numbers. In front
of her was a round cage filled with
numbered balls in different colours. To
one side stood a table piled with prizes.
Bertie ran his eye over them eagerly.
There was a picnic set
(boring), a toaster
(boring), a hairdryer
(very boring) and
… Bertie almost
leaped out of his
seat – a silver
stunt scooter!
He'd been
begging his
parents to buy
him one since Christmas. Eugene had

one, so did Royston Rich (with his name in gold letters). If he had a stunt scooter, Bertie could learn tricks – back flips, twists and double somersaults. He'd be the Stunt King of the world. But only if he won the scooter. He glanced around. What if someone else got their hands on it before him?

Nick spoke in his ear.

"See anything you want?"

"Not really," Bertie lied. "The prizes are all pretty boring."

"Yes, apart from one," smiled Nick. "I saw you drooling over the scooter."

Bertie frowned. He should have been more careful. "You'd be useless on a scooter," he said.

"Actually I've always wanted one," said Nick.

"Since when?"

"Since this evening," said Nick.

"Well, forget it, because that scooter's mine," warned Bertie.

Nick smirked. "Not if I win it first!"

"No chance," said Bertie.

"Want a bet?" said Nick. "Tonight's my lucky night."

Bertie scowled. Nick could never ride a stunt scooter in a million years. He'd probably run over his own foot. The only reason he wanted one was to spite Bertie. Well, they'd soon see about that. From what Gran had told him bingo was a piece of cake. All he had to do was collect a few numbers and the scooter would be his.

Miss Boot rose to her feet. The first game was about to start.

CHAPTER 3

"I'm sure many of you have played bingo before," said Miss Boot. "As you know, it's a simple game of chance."

"*Fat* chance in your case," muttered Nick.

"In a moment I will call out the numbers," Miss Boot went on. "The first person to cross off every

number on their card is the winner.
They can come forward and choose one
of our marvellous prizes."

Bingo cards were handed out to
every table. Bertie studied the rows of
numbers.

"Good luck, Bertie!" whispered Nick.
"Let me know if you need any help."

Bertie stuck out his tongue.

Miss Boot turned a handle, making the
coloured balls bounce inside their cage.

CLUNK! PLOP! One of them rolled
down the chute.

"Number four – knock on the door!"
Miss Boot shouted.

Bertie searched the numbers on his
bingo card. Rats! No number four. He

glanced at Nick, who seemed more interested in sneaking a sweet from his grandma's handbag.

"Ooh, lucky for some!" Julia giggled, marking her card with a pencil.

The cage spun round and another ball shot out. "Forty-four – droopy drawers!" cried Miss Boot.

Bertie couldn't see what her pants had to do with it, but forty-four wasn't on his card.

Dirty Bertie

The game went on. Bertie's luck improved. He'd managed to cross off nine numbers on his card. Only six more to go and he would win.

Miss Boot held up the next ball. "Twenty-six – pick and mix!"

"BINGO!" someone whooped.

Bertie looked up. Nick's grandma was on her feet, waving her card in the air.

Dirty Bertie

"You're kidding!" groaned Bertie.

"I don't believe it," moaned Gran.

"Tough luck, Bertie!" jeered Nick. "You snooze, you lose!"

Bertie watched Nick's grandma go forward as people started to clap.

"That's SO unfair," muttered Gran. "She doesn't even *like* bingo!"

Nick's grandma inspected the prizes.

Not the scooter, please not the scooter, Bertie thought to himself.

Julia's hand hovered for a moment – then she chose the picnic set and carried it back to her seat. Bertie breathed a sigh of relief.

Miss Boot announced that they would take a short break for drinks and pizza.

Dirty Bertie

Bertie found himself in the queue behind Know-All Nick.

"Your grandma's so lucky," said Bertie, helping himself to a slice of pizza.

Nick smirked. "You think it's luck?"

"What else do you call it?" asked Bertie.

"Skill," said Nick. "I can tell you why she won."

"Why?" said Bertie.

Nick looked round then lowered his voice. "Because I have power over Miss Boot," he whispered. "It's called mind control."

Bertie rolled his eyes. "You're such a liar!"

"That's what you think," bragged Nick.

Dirty Bertie

"You won't be laughing when I win the next game."

Bertie watched his enemy bite into a big slice of pepperoni pizza. *He's making it up*, he thought. Nick could only control Miss Boot's mind if he had superpowers. And even if he did, the balls were chosen by pure chance. All the same, Nick's grandma *had* won the first game. Bertie decided he'd have to keep a close eye on that two-faced sneak.

CHAPTER 4

Miss Boot took her seat and the next round began.

RATTLE-RATTLE-PLOP! Another ball whizzed down the chute.

"Sixty-two! Tickety boo!" cried Miss Boot.

"YES!" said Bertie, crossing off the number. He glanced over at Nick, who

was taking another
sweet from his
grandma's bag. He
didn't even seem to
be paying attention.

"Eighty-five – staying
alive!" boomed Miss
Boot.

Result! thought Bertie –
two out of two. At this rate he'd soon
cross off every number. Wouldn't Nick
turn green when he walked off with
the scooter? Mind control – as if! For a
moment there Nick had almost had him
fooled!

The balls spun round and dropped
down the chute. Miss Boot called out

one number after another. Bertie was so
excited he was bouncing up and down
in his seat. Just two more numbers
and he would win! *Nine or forty-one*, he
prayed, fixing his eyes on Miss Boot.

PLOP! The next coloured ball shot
down the chute. Miss Boot held it up.

Dirty Bertie

"Twenty-two – two little ducks!" she shouted.

"BINGO!" yelled a voice.

Bertie sunk his head onto the table. No! Please! Anyone but Know-All Nick!

Nick stood up and patted him on the back. "Like I said, Bertie, mind control!" he grinned.

Bertie could hardly bear to watch. Miss Boot checked the winning card and led Nick over to the table to choose his prize. Nick made a big deal of taking his time, enjoying Bertie's torture. He looked at the toaster and picked up the hairdryer. At last he chose his prize – the stunt scooter.

"It's so unfair!" groaned Bertie.

Dirty Bertie

Gran shook her head. "I know!" she said. "What are the chances of them *both* winning?"

Bertie sat up. It was a good question. It was almost as if Nick *knew* which numbers would come up. But that wasn't possible … was it? Bertie noticed Nick had left something on his chair – his grandma's handbag. She had seen it too and tried to grab it. But Bertie got there first.

"Hey, give that back!" she cried.

Wait a minute, what was this? Bertie found sheets of sticky-backed numbers hidden among the sweets! He leaped to his feet.

"HE CHEATED!" he yelled.

"BERTIE!" snapped Miss Boot. "SIT DOWN!"

"But he did, Miss!" said Bertie. "He's been sticking numbers on his card."

"I haven't!" whined Nick, turning pink.

Nick's grandma stood up.

"Really! Some people are such bad losers."

"If you don't believe me, look in the bag!" said Bertie, holding it up.

Miss Boot was losing patience. "Let me see that," she said.

Bertie went over to the stage and gave her the bag. Miss Boot looked at the sheets of sticky numbers, then at Nick's winning card. On a closer look, she found many of the numbers could be peeled off. She screwed up the piece of paper.

"NICHOLAS!" she thundered.

Nick let out a wail. "It wasn't my fault!"

"Then whose fault was it?" asked Miss Boot.

"My grandma's," bleated Nick. "It was her idea!"

People gasped and turned their heads.

Dirty Bertie

"Don't tell lies!" said Julia.

"I'm not!" squawked Nick. "You said that no one would find out."

"THAT'S ENOUGH!" barked Miss Boot. "You should both be ashamed of yourselves! Give back your prizes right now."

Nick and his grandma did as they were told. As they left the stage they found rows of angry faces staring at them.

"BOO! CHEATS!" cried someone. Others joined in.

Nick and his grandma didn't wait to hear more. They grabbed their things and fled from the hall, banging the door behind them.

Miss Boot shook her head. "Well, Bertie," she said. "For once I must thank you for interrupting."

"That's okay," said Bertie. "But what about their prizes?"

Miss Boot thought for a moment. She could return them to the table, but there was only half an hour left and they'd have prizes left over. It seemed a terrible waste. "I guess *someone* should have them," she said. "I don't suppose you like scooters?"

"LIKE THEM?" gasped Bertie.

He could hardly believe his luck – and to think he almost hadn't come! He couldn't wait to zoom into school on his new stunt scooter on Monday morning. It turned out Gran had been right all along – bingo was the greatest game ever!

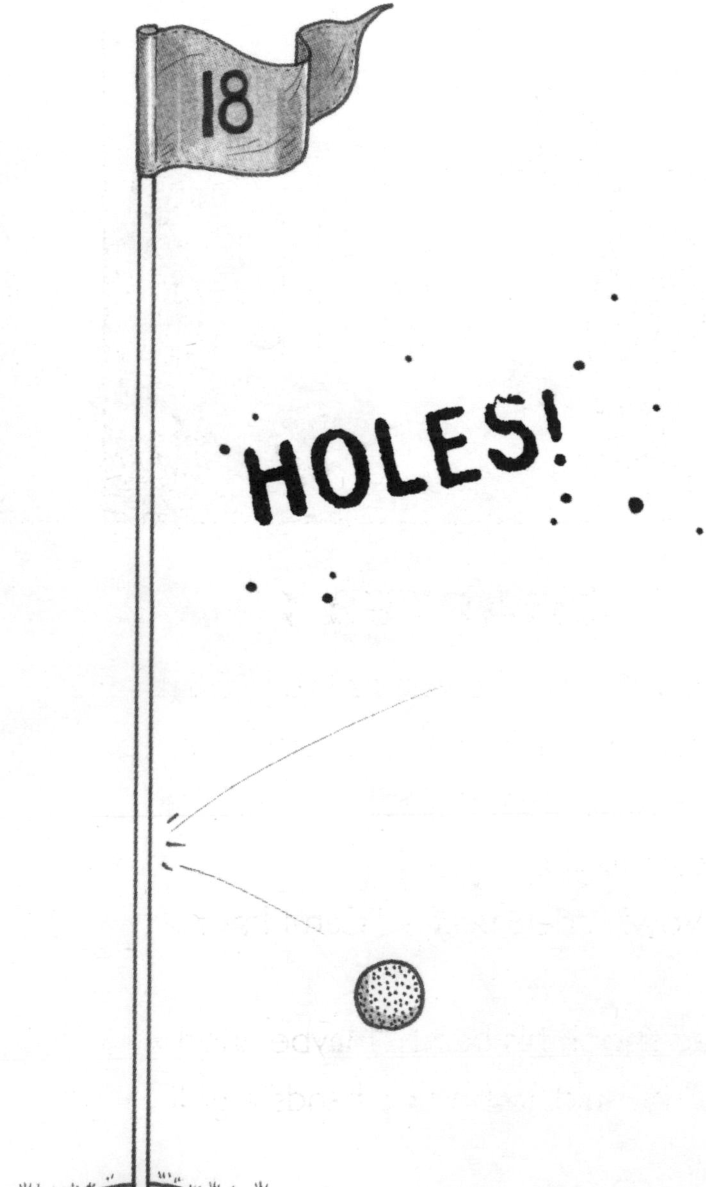
18
HOLES!

CHAPTER 1

Bertie watched the golf ball roll across the lawn and into the small black cup.

WHIRR-CLICK-PLOCK!

It spat it out.

"Wow!" cried Bertie. "Can I have a go?"

Dad shook his head. "Maybe another time," he said. In Bertie's hands a golf club was a dangerous weapon.

"Please," begged Bertie. "Just one little go!"

Dad sighed. "All right, but for goodness' sake take it easy."

Bertie gripped the club and took careful aim.

"Gently," warned Dad.

Bertie swung the golf club.

THWUCK!

The ball flew like a missile and cannoned off the garden wall.

"ARGH!" Dad ducked as it zoomed past his head and buried itself in the hedge.

"HA, HA! Good shot, Bertie!" Bertie looked round to see Royston Rich getting out of his dad's sports car. Royston got on Bertie's nerves. His head

was so big you'd think his dad would
need a larger car.

"What do *you* want?" asked Bertie.

"Oh, we were just passing by," said
Royston. "Actually we've been playing at
Dad's golf club!"

Mr Rich put a hand on his son's
shoulder. "I'm a member at Pudsley Hills,"
he said. "On the committee, in fact."

Dad rolled his eyes. "You don't say."

"Dad's *awesome* at golf," bragged Royston. "He's won tons of trophies."

Mr Rich chuckled. "I am pretty good, though I say so myself." He turned to Dad. "I didn't know you played, old man."

"Oh yes," said Dad. "I'm not bad – though I say so myself."

"Really?" Mr Rich smiled, smoothing his moustache. "Well, we should have a game sometime."

"Anytime you like," said Dad.

"Super. Next Sunday then?"

"You're on."

Bertie couldn't believe his ears. A golf match against Mr Rich – surely that was asking for trouble? Still, he didn't want to miss all the fun.

"Can I come?" he begged.

"Why not?" said Mr Rich. "The boys

can act as our caddies."

"Fine by me," said Dad.

"Me too," said Bertie, wondering what a caddy could be.

Mr Rich strolled back to his car.
"By the way, a little tip," he said to Dad.
"Don't lift your head when you play the ball."

"See you Bertie! You are *so* going to lose," sneered Royston, sticking out his tongue.

"Get lost, goofy!" said Bertie.

Mr Rich drove off with a screech of tyres.

Bertie frowned at his dad. "I thought you hated him?" he said.

"Maurice Rich? Can't stand the man," said Dad.

"So why play golf with him?"

"To beat him, of course," said Dad. "It's time I taught that snooty show-off a lesson."

CHAPTER 2

Over supper Bertie mentioned who they'd run into that morning.

"Maurice Rich?" groaned Mum. "What did he want?"

"Nothing," said Dad.

"He wants to play Dad at golf," said Bertie.

Suzy stopped eating. Mum narrowed

her eyes.

"You're not serious?" she said.

Dad shrugged. "It's only a game."

"Oh yes!" scoffed Suzy. "That's what you said last time!"

Bertie hadn't forgotten last time. On Sports Day both dads had joined in the Parent-Child race. It had ended in an ugly brawl.

"He challenged me," said Dad. "You know what a pompous twerp he is!"

"So ignore him," said Mum. "Honestly, you're worse than a pair of kids."

"I could hardly say no. He saw me practising," argued Dad.

"For the first time in ages," said Mum. "Your clubs have probably gone rusty."

Bertie wiped his nose. "I'm good at golf," he said.

"You've never played," said Suzy.

"I have! On holiday, remember?"

Suzy rolled her eyes. "That was crazy golf, dumbo."

"It's still golf," said Bertie. "And actually it's a lot harder 'cos there's castles and stuff in the way."

Dad shook his head. "This is *real* golf, Bertie, on a proper golf course. And if you're my caddy, you'll have to behave."

Suzy giggled. "You're taking Bertie?"

"I'd be more use than you," said Bertie. "Anyway, what *is* a caddy?"

"It's a sort of helper," explained Dad. "You carry my golf bag and hand me a club when I need one."

Bertie frowned. "Can't I do potting?"

"It's called putting," sighed Dad. "And no, you can't. Your job is to do what I tell you and not get in the way."

Bertie pushed some peas round his plate. What was the point of going if he wasn't allowed to *do* anything? He wanted to beat the Riches just as much as Dad – after all, he'd be the one to suffer if they lost. Royston would brag about it for months.

CHAPTER 3

Bertie stared out of the window as they
pulled into the car park. Royston and
his dad were waiting by the clubhouse,
wearing matching outfits – red jumpers,
yellow trousers and white golf caps.
Bertie thought they looked like two giant
sticks of rock.

Mr Rich's golf bag was almost as big

as him and stuffed with shiny new clubs.
Beside it, Dad's bag looked like it came
from a charity shop.

"Morning!" said Mr Rich. "How about
a little bet to make this interesting?
Twenty pounds?"

"Make it thirty," said Dad.

Mr Rich chuckled. "Suits me, if you
want to lose your money."

Thirty pounds? Bertie's mouth hung
open. That was practically a year's
pocket money! He hoped Dad knew
what he was doing.

Mr Rich put his bag in the back of a
golf buggy and climbed in beside Royston.
"See you at the first hole!" he called.

Dad nodded. "Where'd you get the
buggy?"

"Oh, didn't I say, old man? We took

Dirty Bertie

the last one," grinned Mr Rich. "Never mind, I'm sure you'll enjoy the walk!" He threw them a wave and drove off.

"It's not fair!" grumbled Bertie. "Why do *they* get a buggy and not us?"

"It's healthier to walk," snapped Dad. "Bring the trolley."

Bertie dragged the trolley behind him. It had one squeaky wheel. He kept tipping it too far and spilling golf clubs everywhere.

Dirty Bertie

Royston and Mr Rich were waiting for them at the first hole. Bertie stared.

"Where's the golf course?" he said.

"This is it," said Dad.

"But it's just grass and trees! I can't even see the hole!" moaned Bertie.

Dad pointed to a tiny red flag in the distance.

"That's *miles* away!" cried Bertie. "It'll take forever!"

Mr Rich cleared his throat. "Are we playing or not?" he said.

"Sorry," said Dad. "Go ahead."

Mr Rich stood over his ball. He swung back his club.

PLINK!

The ball flew straight down the middle of the fairway.

Dad was next. He placed his ball,

Dirty Bertie

stood over it and waggled the club.
Then he swished the air a few times.

"Aren't you meant to hit it?" asked
Bertie.

Dad glared. "I'm *going to* if you'll
shut up."

PLUNK!

The ball swerved left and vanished
into a thick clump of trees.

"Oh, bad luck, old man!" smirked
Mr Rich. Bertie shot his dad a look of
disgust. The least he could do was hit
the ball straight.

Royston climbed into the golf buggy
beside his dad.

"See you up at the green – if you ever
get there!" he sniggered.

By the time they reached the green,
Bertie's legs were aching. The Riches
were waiting for them.

Mr Rich putted his ball and watched it
go in.

"We win the hole!" whooped
Royston.

Dad filled in the score-card.

"Come on," he said to Bertie. "And
stop dropping all the clubs."

"It's not *my* fault, it's this stupid
trolley," grumbled Bertie. "If we had
a buggy I wouldn't have to drag it
everywhere."

CHAPTER 4

The game went on for hour after hour. By the time they reached the twelfth hole, Bertie felt like they'd been playing for days.

Royston climbed out of his buggy. "You're lucky we're only four up!" he boasted.

"Up where?" asked Bertie.

Dirty Bertie

"Four holes ahead, stupid," said
Royston. "And there's only six holes left
to play."

Six holes! Bertie didn't think he could
bear it. He had walked about a hundred
miles. He'd hunted in woods, poked
in bushes and slipped over in a muddy
stream. The Riches meanwhile had sailed
round the course in their golf buggy.
Royston was now at the wheel and he
zoomed off as if he was driving a Ferrari.

Mr Rich placed his ball. "Winner goes
first, so that's me again," he said.

PLINK!

The ball rose into the air – another
perfect drive down the middle.

PLUNK!

Dirty Bertie

Dad's ball skidded left and vanished into the long grass. He groaned.

"Oh dear! Looks like it's just not your day," chuckled Mr Rich.

Dad stomped off to look for his ball.

Let's face it, we're going to lose, thought Bertie. CRASH! The trolley tipped over for the hundredth time, dumping the clubs on the grass. Bertie sighed and stood it up. *Wait a minute, what was this in the zip pocket?* Loads of golf balls! Why hadn't Dad mentioned this before? They could have saved so much time!

Bertie took one of the balls and dropped it on a patch of grass.

Dirty Bertie

"Dad! Over here!" he yelled.

Dad came hurrying back.

"Is that my ball?" he frowned.

"Of course. I just found it," said Bertie.

Dad scratched his head. 'That's odd, I thought it went over there. Still, I'm not complaining."

He hit a shot, which bounced three times and rolled on to the green.

Maurice Rich looked like he might die of shock. Dad putted his ball and went on to win the hole.

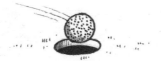

At the next hole Mr Rich seemed a little on edge. He gripped his club and drew it back.

"Is that a lake?" asked Bertie, pointing to the right.

Dirty Bertie

Mr Rich lowered his club. "I was just about to play," he snapped.

"Oh sorry, go on," said Bertie.

Mr Rich swung his club back again…

"Only I was just wondering, do they have lakes in golf?" asked Bertie.

"YES, IT'S A LAKE!" said Mr Rich through gritted teeth.

"What happens if your ball goes in?" asked Bertie.

"You take an extra shot and have to play again," snarled Mr Rich. "Now if you will please BE QUIET…"

Dirty Bertie

Mr Rich swung. The ball sliced to the right and landed in the lake with a plop.

Dad grinned. "Bad luck, old man!" he said.

Bertie decided that golf only made people bad-tempered. It certainly had that effect on Mr Rich. One of his shots hit a tree. He covered himself in sand trying to hit his ball out of a bunker. When he missed a putt he yelled at Royston for breathing too loudly. The next three holes all went to Bertie's dad.

When they reached the final hole the scores were level. But Mr Rich hadn't finished. He hit a perfect shot, which

came to rest ten paces from the flag.
Dad's shot landed a little short of the
green.

Royston gave Bertie a look of
triumph. One good putt and the game
was theirs. Royston zoomed past and
parked his golf buggy on the slope
above the green.

Mr Rich stood over his ball.

"This is to win the match then," he
said smugly.

Bertie wasn't watching. "Mr Rich!" he
said.

"Not now!" snapped Mr Rich.

"But I think you…"

"WILL YOU SHUT UP!" growled
Mr Rich.

He drew his club slowly back.
PLOCK!

Dirty Bertie

The ball rolled straight towards the hole. It might have got there but for one thing – Royston had left the brake off the golf buggy. It was bumping down the slope on to the green. It picked up speed, heading straight for Mr Rich's ball.

"NO! STOP IT!" screeched Mr Rich. "STOP…"

Dirty Bertie

CRUNCH!

The ball was squashed under the front wheel. To play it Mr Rich would have needed a shovel.

"ROYSTON, YOU IDIOT!" he roared, his face purple.

Dirty Bertie

Twenty minutes later Bertie and Dad were enjoying the All-Day Breakfast at the golf-club restaurant. Mr Rich's thirty pound bet was paying the bill.

"I still can't believe I won," said Dad.

"Only because you had a brilliant caddy," said Bertie.

"True," said Dad. "If you hadn't found my lost ball, I'd have been in trouble."

"Yes, lucky I looked in your bag," said Bertie.

Dad put down his fork. "My bag? You mean that *wasn't* my ball?"

"It was one of them," said Bertie. "I found it in the pocket of your bag."

"But it wasn't the ball I lost?"

"Oh no," said Bertie. "I gave up

looking for that."

Dad gasped. "But you can't just swap balls!" he said. "You're meant to take an extra shot. IT'S CHEATING!"

"Is it?" said Bertie.

"Of course it is!"

Bertie shrugged. "Oh well, it's a stupid game. Are you leaving that sausage?"

Dirty Bertie

RATS!

For Tim and Sarah ~ D R

For Mark and Sarah – wishing you a long and happy married life together! ~ A M

Contents

CHAPTER 1

"Did you know rats eat their own poo?" asked Bertie, over breakfast.

Suzy pulled a face. "MUM! Bertie's being disgusting!" she moaned.

"I'm not," said Bertie. "I saw it on TV. Rats are amazing. You can flush them down the toilet and they still survive!"

"We don't want to know, Bertie,"

sighed Mum.

Bertie poured Puffo Pops into his bowl. He didn't see why no one liked rats. Actually they were a whole lot cleaner than humans. You didn't see humans picking fleas off each other.

"You're dropping cereal everywhere," said Suzy.

Bertie looked down to see a trail of Puffo Pops on the table.

"It's not my fault," he said. "There's a hole in this box."

Mum took it from him. It looked like the corner of the box had been nibbled away.

"Did you do this, Bertie?" asked Mum.

"No – why do I always get the blame?" asked Bertie.

Mum frowned. Getting down on her knees she poked her head into the cupboard.

"Oh no!" she groaned. "MICE!"

"Where?" cried Bertie.

"There," said Mum. "Those are mouse droppings!"

"EWWW!" cried Suzy, putting down her spoon.

Bertie went over to look. He had never seen mouse droppings before. They were small brown pellets, a bit like hamster or rat droppings.

"Don't touch them!" warned Mum. "They're covered in germs – you'll catch something!"

Dad came in as they were taking all the tins out of the cupboard. "What's going on?" he asked.

"We've got mice," said Mum.

"You're joking!"

"No," said Bertie. "They've left tiny poos in the cupboard. Have a look!"

"No thanks," said Dad. "Are you sure it's mice?"

"It could be rats," said Bertie, hopefully.

"It's definitely mice,' said Mum,

standing up. "The question is, what do we do about it?"

"I like mice," said Bertie. "Can I keep one?"

"NO!" shouted Mum and Dad at once.

"Why not?"

"Because mice are pests," said Mum. "They nest in the walls."

"Once they move in they start having babies," warned Dad.

"REALLY?" said Bertie.

This sounded brilliant. He would have liked a rat but a mouse was the next best thing – and baby mice would be even better! He could train them to play mouse football or to juggle lumps of cheese.

"Right," said Dad. "I'll get some poison."

"POISON!" howled Bertie.

"That's cruel!" said Suzy.

"And dangerous too," said Mum. "What if Whiffer eats it?"

Dad hadn't thought of that. Whiffer ate anything he found on the floor.

"Okay. Then I'll buy a mousetrap," said Dad.

"What for?" moaned Bertie. "I said I'll look after them!"

"How many times do I have to tell you – mice are not pets!" said Mum.

"They are, Trevor's got one," Bertie argued.

"I don't care," said Mum. "We are NOT having mice in the house."

"They're disgusting," said Dad. "They eat all the food and leave their mess everywhere."

Dirty Bertie

Bertie didn't see why everyone was making such a big fuss. Mice had to poo somewhere. Besides, if he had a pet mouse he'd make sure it was house-trained. He would make it a teeny-weeny toilet the size of a matchbox.

"Please!" he begged. "Just one little mouse."

"NO!" said Mum firmly. "No mice and that's the end of the matter."

CHAPTER 2

When Dad got home from work he had
something to show them.

"There we are, one mousetrap," he
said, putting it on the table.

Bertie stared. He'd never seen a
mousetrap before. It was a flat wooden
block with a metal handle on a spring.
It came with instructions.

"What does it mean, 'snap'?" Bertie wanted to know.

"That's how it works," said Dad. "I'll show you." He pulled the metal handle back until it clicked. "The mouse comes sniffing around and smells the bait," he explained. "Sooner or later he hops up here to take a nibble and…"

SNAP! The metal handle flew back as he poked it with a pencil.

Bertie stared. "But that's horrible! You'll kill it!" he argued.

"I certainly hope so," said Mum.

"That's the point. It's a mousetrap," said Dad.

"But can't you just catch it, then let it go outside?" Bertie pleaded.

Mum shook her head. "We don't want it coming back, we want to get rid of it once and for all."

Bertie scowled at the mousetrap. "Well, I think it's murder," he said. "And don't blame me if a ghost mouse comes back to haunt you."

Dirty Bertie

Upstairs Bertie lay on his bed, thinking. It
wasn't fair – what had the mouse ever
done to them? If it was up to him he'd
think of a way to catch the mouse alive.
Bertie sat up suddenly. Yes, why not?
He could make his own mousetrap.
He went to his wardrobe and pulled out
an old shoebox from under his clothes.

Dirty Bertie

Twenty minutes later he put down
the scissors and admired his work.

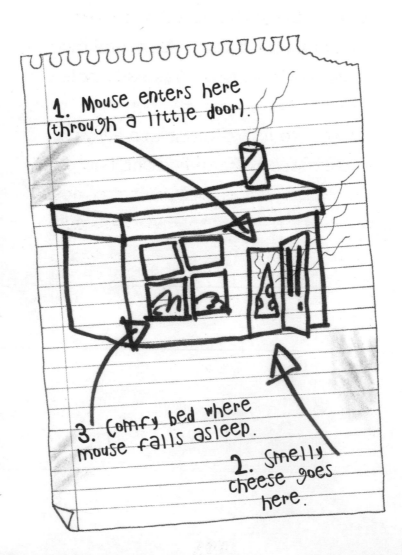

Dirty Bertie

Bertie had it all planned. He'd wait
till everyone was asleep and then sneak
down to the kitchen. Dad's nasty old
mousetrap could go in the bin and the
Super-Safe Mouse Catcher would take
its place.

Bertie would have to get up early
tomorrow morning to find out if his plan
had worked. It was probably better not
to mention anything to Mum and Dad.
The mouse could live under his bed –
at least until he had house-trained it,
anyway.

CHAPTER 3

Bertie woke up. Light was spilling through his bedroom curtains. What time was it? Oh no! He shot out of bed – he had to get down to the kitchen before anyone else.

Downstairs the Super-Safe Mouse Catcher was still where he'd left it. Bertie tiptoed closer and kneeled

down. Holding his breath, he listened
for mousey squeaks. Nothing. He lay
on his belly and peeped through the
tiny doorway. The lump of cheese had
vanished. But there, asleep in a heap
of tissue paper, was something small,
brown and furry.

Dirty Bertie

Bertie could hardly believe it. His mouse catcher had actually worked! Wait till he told Darren and Eugene about this! Carefully he lifted the shoebox and scooped up the sleepy little mouse. It twitched in his hand. Just then he heard footsteps on the stairs. Someone was coming! Quickly he replaced the mouse, jammed on the lid and hid the box behind his back.

"Oh Bertie! You're up early," said Mum.

"Yes, I was just um … getting a drink," said Bertie. "I'm going back to bed now."

Mum frowned. "What's that?" she said.

"What?"

"That thing you're hiding behind your back."

"Oh this," said Bertie, bringing out the shoebox. "It's, you know … just a box."

Dirty Bertie

Mum folded her arms. "What's in it?"

"Nothing!" said Bertie.

The lid moved. The mouse must have woken up. Mum was staring at the box.

"Open it," she said.

Bertie sighed. It was no use arguing, he'd been rumbled. He removed the lid.

Mum peeped inside. "EEEEK!"

Dirty Bertie

"SHH! You'll scare him!" said Bertie. "He's only just woken up."

"It's a mouse!" said Mum. "Where did you get him?"

Bertie proudly explained how he'd made the Super-Safe Mouse Catcher where he'd found Monty asleep.

"Monty?" said Mum.

"That's his name," said Bertie. "Isn't he cute? Look at his little paws!"

Mum shook her head. "I know what you're after, Bertie, but you are not keeping him."

"He's tiny! He won't be any trouble!" pleaded Bertie.

"NO!" said Mum. "He's got to go."

Bertie looked sadly at Monty, who was now sniffing around his box.

Dirty Bertie

"I won't let him out," he promised.
"He can stay in my bedroom!"

"Not a chance," said Mum. "Take him outside and let him go. And don't do it anywhere near the house!"

Bertie took the box to the back door. It wasn't fair. He never got to keep any of his pets. Even when he tried to keep dog fleas his mum squashed them. He went outside. Mum had said to release Monty away from the house, but where exactly? If the mouse got next door, the Nicelys' mean old cat might catch him.

Bertie looked round the garden. Where would be safest? The flower beds? The vegetable patch? No, of

Dirty Bertie

course, the shed! It wasn't near the
house and better still it was filled with
piles of junk. Nobody would notice a
tiny little mouse house hidden under a
blanket. If he was careful he could visit
Monty every day!

CHAPTER 4

Next morning, after breakfast, Bertie sneaked out to the shed. He'd saved Monty some peanut butter on toast.

"Monty! Monty?" he called.

He lifted up an old blanket to uncover the shoebox.

"You stay here, Monty," he explained, feeding him bits of toast. "I've got to go to school, but I'll see you later."

He watched the mouse nibble his breakfast. It seemed a pity to leave him all alone. Then Bertie had an interesting thought. He looked down at his school bag. The shoebox would just about fit inside. He could cover it with his PE kit and Miss Boot would never suspect a thing.

On the way to school Bertie met up with Darren and Eugene.

"You'll never guess what I've got in my bag," he said, grinning.

"What?" said Eugene.

Bertie took off his backpack and pulled out the shoebox. Carefully he lifted the lid.

Darren and Eugene peered inside.

Monty blinked up at them.

"A mouse!" gasped Darren. "Where'd you get him?"

"I caught him," said Bertie, proudly. "We found mouse droppings in our kitchen so I made my own mouse catcher. He's called Monty."

"Cool," said Eugene. "What are you going to do with him?"

"Keep him," said Bertie. "He's coming to school."

Eugene stared. "Miss Boot will go bonkers. Have you forgotten she's terrified of rats?"

"So what? He's a mouse," said Bertie.

"Same thing," said Darren. "She'll go nuts if she sees him."

"She won't," said Bertie, closing the lid. "He can stay in here and we'll take him out at break to play with him."

Later that morning Miss Boot was droning on about living in Tudor times. Bertie thought she was probably old enough to remember them. He hadn't checked on Monty for at least ten minutes. Reaching into his bag, he brought out the shoebox and took off the lid.

YIKES! Where was Monty?

Bertie emptied the contents of his bag on to the floor. Lunch box, pencils, socks, mouse droppings … but no mouse.

"What's up?" hissed Darren.

"He's escaped!" said Bertie.

"Who has?"

"Monty, you dumbo! He's not in his box."

They passed the message to Eugene and the three of them searched under their desks. No luck. Darren nudged Bertie and pointed to the front.

"What?" hissed Bertie.

"There! On Miss Boot's desk," said Darren.

Bertie stared in horror. A neat trail of mouse droppings led across Miss Boot's desk to Monty, who sat there nibbling the register. Bertie had to do something before it was too late. He jumped to his feet.

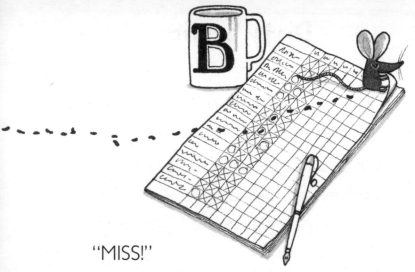

"MISS!"

Miss Boot glared at him. "What is it now, Bertie?"

"I've lost my ... er ... my pen!" said Bertie.

"Well, borrow one from someone else," sighed Miss Boot.

"But it's my best pen, I need to look for it," begged Bertie.

"SIT DOWN!" thundered Miss Boot.

Bertie sat down. Monty had vanished from the teacher's desk. Where had he got to now? Bertie caught sight of something streaking across the floor.

Dirty Bertie

"Now," said Miss Boot. "I want you to write down this— AARGHHH!"

She gave a yelp. Something was tickling her ankle. The ticklish feeling crept up the back of her leg. She tried to ignore it…

"I want you to write this— OOOH … HEE-HAA!" she squawked.

The class stood up to get a better view. Their teacher was dancing around as if her pants were on fire. Something brown and furry shot up her skirt.

"AARGGHHH! A RAT!" she screamed.

Bertie wouldn't have believed that Miss Boot could move so fast. One moment she was hopping around like a jumping bean – the next she had leapt on to her desk.

"A RAT! A RAT!" she shrieked. "DO SOMETHING!" This was Bertie's chance. He grabbed the shoebox and leaped into action. A mad chase broke out as Bertie scrambled under chairs and tables and Monty tried to escape.

At last he managed to get Monty back in the box.

"It's okay, Miss, I've got him," Bertie

panted. "He can't get away."

Slowly Miss Boot climbed down off her desk and smoothed out her skirt. She shuddered.

"I hate rats!" she said.

"But he's not a rat, he's a mouse," said Bertie. "His name's Monty."

Miss Boot turned her head. She gave Bertie a long hard look.

"And how exactly do you know his name?" she demanded.

Bertie gulped. *Ooops! Now he really was in trouble.*

RUNNER!

CHAPTER 1

Bertie sat down and pulled off his trainers with a groan. He thought PE was meant to be fun. Somebody should tell Miss Boot that. She'd just put them through an hour of star jumps, squats and sit-ups.

"It is obvious that many of you are not fit," she said. "Too many crisps and

too much TV. What you need is fresh
air – that's why this Friday we are going
to be doing cross-country."

Bertie rolled his eyes. What new form
of torture was this?

"Who can tell me what cross-country
is?" asked Miss Boot.

Know-All Nick was bouncing up and
down as if he might burst. "Miss, Miss

Dirty Bertie

I know!" he panted. "Is it like a race?"

"Very good, Nicholas," said Miss Boot. "Cross-country is a race run over fields and paths. Who'd like to try it?"

Class 3 looked at the floor.

"I see," said Miss Boot. "And who'd rather stay inside and practise one hundred spellings?"

No one spoke.

Dirty Bertie

"Good, then remember to bring your PE kit on Friday. What do you need on Friday, Bertie?"

"Um … sandwiches?" said Bertie.

"PE KIT!" thundered Miss Boot. "Do NOT forget! Next month it's the County Cross-Country Trials and we will be taking part. I want four good runners for the team."

Bertie didn't know where Miss Boot was going to find them. Most of the class were slower than a tortoise with a limp. Trevor Trembleton usually brought a note when it came to PE and Know-All Nick was weedier than a stick insect. Nick was the only boy Bertie knew who could play football without getting mud on his kit.

CHAPTER 2

At break time Bertie and his friends
leaned against the railings.

"Cross-country," sighed Eugene. "Isn't
that really tough?"

"Don't ask me," said Bertie. "Why
can't we do something fun like beach
volleyball?"

Bertie had seen beach volleyball on TV.

It looked brilliant, but the school didn't have a beach — or a volleyball, for that matter.

"Anyway," said Darren. "At least we won't be in the cross-country team. Miss Boot will pick the fastest runners."

"I don't know, I'm pretty speedy," said Bertie.

"Pretty *weedy*, you mean," said a voice.

Bertie looked round to see his old enemy, Know-All Nick. Didn't he have anything better to do than listen in on other people's conversations?

"Mind your own business," said Bertie.

Nick took no notice. "Since when were you a fast runner?" he sneered.

Bertie stuck out his chin. "I'm faster than you."

"Really? Who was first back to the coach after swimming last time?" said Nick. "Oh yes, it was me!"

"Only because you cheated," said Bertie. "I'd like to see you do cross-country. You couldn't cross the road."

"Actually, I'm probably the fittest in the class," boasted Nick. "Because I eat all my vegetables!"

"You look like a vegetable," said Bertie.

"You smell like one," replied Nick. "Anyway, I bet I could beat you."

"No chance," said Bertie.

Dirty Bertie

"Want to bet?" said Nick. "First one to cross the finish line wins."

"You're on," said Bertie, shaking hands.

"And the loser…" Nick thought for a minute. "The loser has to kiss Miss Boot!"

Dirty Bertie

Bertie almost choked. Kiss Miss Boot? He'd rather kiss Angela Nicely! Come to that, he'd rather kiss Darren!

"What's the matter — backing out, scaredy cat?" jeered Nick.

"Course not," said Bertie.

"Good, then I'll see you Friday. Better get in some practice, kissy lips!"

Bertie glared after him.

"Yikes!" said Eugene. "You wouldn't really?"

"What?" said Bertie.

"Kiss Miss Boot?"

"No way," said Bertie. "But I won't have to cos I'm going to win."

"But say you lost," said Darren. "You'd actually have to kiss her. I mean, Miss Boot!"

"Okay, stop going on about it!" said

Bertie. He was starting to feel sick. "Anyway, it's only Know-All Nick. He may be the class brainiac but he runs like a penguin. There's no way he'll beat me at cross-country."

Bertie folded his arms. He was almost looking forward to Friday. This time Nick had picked the wrong bet. He'd never been sporty. If you threw him a ball he practically screamed. Five minutes of cross-country and he'd be begging to stop.

Bertie couldn't wait to see Nick try to kiss Miss Boot. She'd probably flatten him with her handbag.

CHAPTER 3

On Friday morning Bertie wolfed down his breakfast. As usual he was late for school.

"Oh, I need my PE kit today," he said.

Mum rolled her eyes. "Why didn't you say so last night?"

"I forgot," said Bertie. "We're doing cross-country with Miss Boot."

Dirty Bertie

Suzy looked up. "You can't be serious!" she said.

"Why not?" said Bertie.

"Do you actually know what cross-country is?" asked Suzy.

"Course I do, it's a sort of race," said Bertie.

"Yes, a race that lasts for HOURS," said Suzy.

"I'm sure it can't be that bad," said Mum. "These socks are filthy, Bertie!"

"I'm telling you, cross-country is murder," said Suzy. "It should be against the law."

"How do you know so much?" asked Bertie.

"Because we did it last year. I almost died," said Suzy. "Bella was off sick for a week!"

Bertie glanced out of the window at the grey sky. Maybe Miss Boot would put off cross-country till another day? Anyway, it was too late to back out now – he had to beat Know-All Nick and win the bet.

Bertie stood on the starting line with the rest of Class 3. A biting wind swept across Deadwood Country Park. The sky had turned black and the first drops of rain were falling. Bertie shivered in his T-shirt and shorts.

"Can't we run somewhere else?" he asked. "Like indoors?"

"Don't be silly," snapped Miss Boot. "It's cross-country, not tiddlywinks."

"But it's raining, Miss," moaned Eugene.

"And muddy!" grumbled Darren.

"A bit of mud never hurt anyone," said Miss Boot. "When I was at school we used to run when we were up to our knees in snow – and we enjoyed it. Now listen, follow the yellow arrows and you can't get lost."

Bertie looked down the hill. "How far is it?" he asked.

"Not far – three kilometres," said Miss Boot.

THREE KILOMETRES? Had Miss Boot lost her mind? On Sports Day they

Dirty Bertie

raced sixty metres and Bertie was out
of breath. They'd never make it back…
They'd die! Where was the ambulance
crew standing by with stretchers?

Know-All Nick pushed in beside
Bertie. His PE kit shone whiter than his
legs and he was wearing mittens.

"Ready for this, Bertie?" he smirked. "I hope you haven't forgotten our little bet. Last one back has to kiss Miss Boot."

"Good luck with that," said Bertie.

He pulled up his shorts, which were flapping in the wind. Nick wouldn't last long. He hated getting cold and dirty, so beating him shouldn't be difficult. Bertie would set off fast and open up a big lead. Then he could take his time and still cross the line first.

Miss Boot raised her arm. "On your marks, get set … GO!"

Class 3 set off down the hill, bunched together like sardines.

"RUN!" roared Miss Boot. "GET A MOVE ON!"

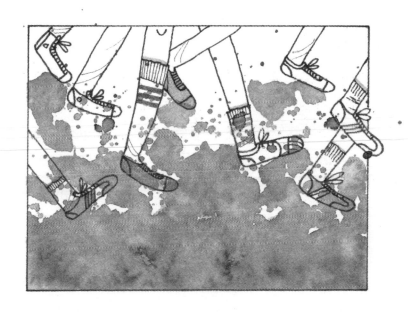

CHAPTER 4

Bertie looked round for Nick. He was tucked in just behind him. They splashed downhill.

At the bottom, the track curved left beside a muddy duck pond. Nick put on a burst of speed to draw level with Bertie. There was barely room for two of them on the path.

Dirty Bertie

Nick pointed. "Look, a crocodile!" he cried.

"Where?" said Bertie, turning his head.

SPLASH!

Nick gave him a violent shove so that he toppled into the pond. The ducks swam round him, quacking in protest.

Dirty Bertie

Bertie clambered out of the pond, dripping wet. He would get Nick for this.

SPLODGE, SPLODGE, SPLODGE!

It took Bertie a while to catch up. His trainers were full of water. He could see his enemy ahead, climbing a steep hill. Nick paused and hung on to a low branch, panting heavily.

"Get a move on, slow coach!" he called.

Bertie hurried up the hill. Nick waited until he drew close, then let go of the branch he was holding.

THWACK! It sprang back, whacking Bertie in the face.

"ARGH!" He slipped and rolled back down the hill.

"HA! HA! No time to lie down, Bertie!" jeered Nick.

Bertie picked himself up. He was now soaked through and muddy as a pig. He would catch up with that two-faced sneak if it killed him. He staggered back up the hill.

Bertie splodged on through the mud. How much further? It felt like he'd been running for days.

Call this sport? thought Bertie. *More*

like torture. He bet none of his teachers did cross-country. The nearest Miss Boot got to exercise was reaching for another biscuit.

He'd lost sight of the other runners. They were probably somewhere up ahead. But where was Know-All Nick? He couldn't be that far ahead could he? What if he was out of the woods – or even close to the finish! Bertie staggered on. If he lost he'd have to KISS Miss Boot – in front of everyone! No, it was too ghastly to imagine.

Wait, there was Nick! He was dragging himself along, looking fit to collapse.

Bertie caught up with him. "Getting tired, Nickerless?" he grinned.

"Never!" panted Nick. "I'm … just …

getting ... started."

The track led through the woods beside a field. There was a large sign on the fence:

PRIVATE PROPERTY – NO ENTRY – KEEP OUT!

Bertie glanced round. He could take a shortcut across the field. The finish line was at the top of the hill. In a few minutes he could be there. Wouldn't Nick turn green when he realized he'd lost? Bertie climbed the fence.

"Wait! Where are you going?" wailed Nick. "That's not the right way!"

"It's the way I'm going," said Bertie. "First to the finish – that was the bet. No one said anything about keeping to the course."

Nick looked round. He didn't want

Dirty Bertie

to get into trouble but he couldn't let
Bertie win. Besides, a shortcut meant the
race would be over quicker.

"Hey! Wait for me!" he yelled.

Dirty Bertie

Bertie jogged across the field, skipping over cowpats. This was easy. Once he saw the finish line he'd sprint, leaving Nick way behind. No contest.

"What is this field anyway?" asked Nick.

Bertie shrugged. "Just a cow field. But luckily there aren' t any ... oh." He gulped. A large herd of cows stood blocking their way. Up close, cows were much bigger than you'd think – and these ones didn't look pleased to see them.

Dirty Bertie

Nick grabbed Bertie's arm. "Let's go back."

"They're only cows," said Bertie. "They're probably scared of us."

"They don't look scared," said Nick. "That one's got horns."

"Which one?" said Bertie.

"That black one there."

Bertie's eyes grew wide. "That isn't a cow," he said. "RUN FOR IT!"

Dirty Bertie

They tore across the field. Bertie
looked behind him. The bull — it was
definitely a bull — was charging after
them with its head down. The ground
shook as it thundered closer.

"Help! Mummy!" wailed Nick.

"Make for the fence!" panted Bertie.
Bertie got there first and dived over,
landing in a puddle.

A moment later Nick
crashed on top
of him.

Dirty Bertie

"ARGH! OWW!"

They didn't stop to look back. They kept running until they passed between two white posts. Bertie crossed the finish line just in front.

Miss Boot stepped out to greet them, beaming happily.

"Well done, Bertie! Third place," she said. "And you were a close fourth, Nicholas."

"Third?" wheezed Bertie.

"Yes, which means you'll both be running for the school cross-country team," said Miss Boot.

Bertie groaned. More cross-country? More cold and rain and slogging through miles of mud? Could anything be worse? Well, actually, come to think of it, there was one thing.

"Oh Nickerless, remember our little bet?" said Bertie. "I won. Isn't there something you'd like to give Miss Boot?"

"Oh? What's that?" demanded Miss Boot.

Nick had gone red. He backed away in horror, then turned and fled. Bertie grinned. Actually, Nick could run pretty fast when he wanted to.

CHAPTER 1

Bertie waited anxiously for the vet to
finish his examination. Mr Cage and
Whiffer were old enemies. But today
Whiffer hadn't whined or even tried to
bolt out of the door.

"You say he doesn't like going for
walks?" asked Mr Cage.

"Not really," said Bertie. "Half the

time he just stops and sits down. I think he expects me to carry him."

"I see," said the vet. "And he's not off his food?"

"Not a bit," answered Dad.

"He eats everything — chips are his favourite," said Bertie.

Mr Cage stood up. "Well there's your problem," he said. "He's too fat."

"FAT?" said Bertie.

"You probably haven't noticed," said Mr Cage. "People often don't when their dogs put on weight."

Dad sighed. "So he's not actually sick or anything?" he said.

"Oh no," replied Mr Cage. "He just eats too much."

Bertie looked relieved.

Fat — was that all?

Bertie had been worried that Whiffer
was ill, with something like measles,
chicken pox or maybe doggy pox. But
it turned out he'd just put on weight.
Come to think of it, Whiffer did spend
hours dozing in front of the TV.

But so what? Loads of pets were a bit
porky. Angela Nicely's cat could hardly
squeeze through the cat flap.

"So what should we do about it?"

Dirty Bertie

Dad asked.

"Put him on a strict diet," said the vet. "Two light meals a day and plenty of healthy walks. Cut out the snacking too."

"Hear that Bertie? No more chips," said Dad.

Bertie nodded. It wasn't always chips anyway — sometimes it was pepperoni pizza.

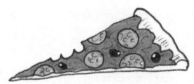

They set off home. Whiffer trailed behind, panting as if he'd just run a marathon. Eventually he sat down and refused to budge.

"Come on!" moaned Bertie, pulling at the lead.

"See?" said Dad. "He's a big lazy lump."

"Don't say that! He'll hear you!" said
Bertie.

"Well it's true – and it's our fault,"
sighed Dad. "Yours especially."

"ME? What did I do?" cried Bertie.

"He's your dog. You should take care
of him," said Dad.

"I do!" argued Bertie. "I'm the one that
feeds him!"

"Yes, and he eats too much," said

Dad. "From tomorrow he starts his diet."

Bertie rolled his eyes. It was all very well saying it, but getting Whiffer to cut down was another matter. He loved eating and he didn't love exercise.

"Come on boy, let's go home," said Bertie.

Whiffer raised a paw and scratched his ear.

"That won't work, you have to order him," said Dad.

"COME ON, WHIFFER! GET A MOVE ON!" Bertie pulled hard on the dog lead. Whiffer got up, walked as far as the next lamp post, then sat down again.

"Hmm," said Bertie. "It might be quicker to carry him."

CHAPTER 2

"Supper's READY!"

Bertie skidded into the kitchen and landed on a chair. "Yum! Sausages and mash!" he said.

"Sit up straight and take your elbows off the table," ordered Mum.

Bertie sighed. He couldn't even sit down without getting in trouble. One

day he was going to open a restaurant
where table manners would be banned.

"So how is Whiffer's diet going?"
asked Dad.

"Fine," said Bertie. "Except he's always
hungry."

"You've got to be firm with him," said
Mum.

"I *am* firm," insisted Bertie.

Something warm was pressing against
his leg. He looked down to discover
Whiffer hiding under the table.

"Where is he anyway?" asked Mum.

"Who?" asked Bertie.

"Whiffer."

Bertie glanced down. "In the garden
probably." Since the diet began Whiffer
wasn't allowed in the kitchen at
mealtimes.

"Anyway I think he's lost weight,"
Bertie said.

Suzy laughed. "I doubt it," she said.

"But he looks thinner – especially
when he's lying down," argued Bertie.

Whiffer was gazing up at him with big
sad eyes. He could smell freshly cooked
sausages – his second favourite food
after chips.

"He's got to learn to cut down," said
Dad.

"He is," said Bertie. "I hardly put
anything in his bowl."

No one was looking. He speared a sausage on his fork and lowered it under the table. Whiffer saw it and licked his lips…

"What are you doing?"

Uh oh – Suzy was staring at him.

"Nothing!" said Bertie.

"You are, you've got something under the table," said Suzy.

Mum leaned down, just in time to see Whiffer wolfing down the last of the sausage.

"BERTIE!" she groaned. "What did we say about feeding him at the table?"

"I couldn't help it," said Bertie. "He was begging me!"

Dad took Whiffer by the collar and led him out. He closed the door behind the dog.

Mum shook her head. "You're not
helping him, Bertie," she said. "Do you
want him to be overweight?"

"No! But he's hungry," said Bertie.

"Greedy more like," said Dad. "He has
to stick to his diet."

Bertie sighed heavily. Whiffer had
only been on his diet for two days but
already it seemed like a year. Whenever
Bertie got back from school Whiffer was

waiting by his dog bowl. He followed Bertie all round the house – even to the toilet. It was driving him up the wall.

"By the way, the Nicelys are coming to supper tomorrow," said Mum.

Suzy groaned. Bertie almost choked on his food.

"What for?" he moaned.

"I invited them," said Mum. "I thought we should get to know them better."

Bertie thought he'd rather get to know the Nicelys less. It was bad enough that they lived next door! Besides, they'd probably bring Angela, who'd want him to play mummies and daddies. He'd just have to keep out of the way till they'd gone.

"Can I eat in my room?" he asked.

"Of course not! You'll eat with us,"

Dirty Bertie

said Mum.

"It won't kill you," said Dad.

"You'd better mind your manners too," warned Mum. "And keep Whiffer out of the way – you know how Mrs Nicely feels about dogs."

Bertie slumped back in his seat. A meal with adoring Angela and her boring parents – could anything be worse?

CHAPTER 3

Bertie looked at the clock. The Nicelys
would be here in half an hour. There
had to be some way to get out of
it. Maybe he could pretend to have
toothache? No, last time he tried that
Mum booked him an appointment with
the dentist. Wait a minute – hadn't
she told him to keep Whiffer out of

the way? That was it! He rushed down to the kitchen, where Mum was busy making supper.

"I just remembered," he said. "Whiffer hasn't had a walk."

"It's too late now," said Mum.

"Can't I just take him round the block?" begged Bertie. "The vet said he needs to go everyday."

"You should have done it earlier," said Mum. "Now go and get changed, and take Whiffer with you. I don't want him in here while there's food around."

Bertie dragged himself upstairs. There was no escape. At least Mum was cooking one of his favourite meals – shepherd's pie. He had seen it on the side, ready to go in the oven.

Once he had changed, Bertie settled

on the lounge sofa to watch TV. Whiffer
hung around, looking pathetic. He'd
finished the food in his bowl and wanted
more. Bertie ignored him – he'd give
up eventually. But ten minutes into the
programme, he looked around. Uh oh –
where was that dopey dog?

Bertie dashed into the kitchen.
Whiffer had his paws on the worktop
and was guzzling something with loud
slurps.

"NO! GET DOWN!" cried Bertie,
pulling him off. He looked at the dish.

AARGHHH! MUM'S SHEPHERD'S
PIE! The one they were having for
supper!

Whiffer looked pleased with himself.
He had gravy round his mouth and a
blob of mashed potato on his nose.

Dirty Bertie

"Bad boy!" said Bertie, wagging a finger. "GO ON! OUT!"

Whiffer ran off. Bertie examined the shepherd's pie. It was a disaster. There was a gaping hole in the middle where Whiffer had been nosing. The smooth mash topping looked like a bomb crater. Bertie put a hand to his head. What on earth was he going to do? Any minute now the Nicelys would arrive and there'd be nothing to give them.

Unless… Bertie thought quickly – maybe the damage could be repaired? First he'd have to fill in the hole. But what with? He looked in the food cupboard. Jam? Porridge? No, of course, peanut butter – brown and easy to spread! He took a spoonful and blobbed it in. Might as well use the whole jar.

Once it was done, he smoothed over the mashed potato to cover his work. The pie still looked like a gloopy mess but it was better than nothing.

Someone was coming. He shoved the pie in the oven and slammed the door, just in time.

Mum looked around. "Where's my shepherd's pie?" she asked.

"Oh, I put it in the oven for you," replied Bertie.

Mum frowned. "I told you not to touch anything," she said, turning the oven up. "And where's that dog? I don't want him here when the Nicelys arrive."

CHAPTER 4

Bertie sat at the table, sandwiched between Suzy and Angela. He ate a spoonful of tomato soup.

Suzy shot him a look. "Don't slurp!" she hissed.

Bertie stuck out his tongue. Angela hadn't stopped talking since she'd arrived but he hadn't listened to a word. He was too worried about the shepherd's pie in the oven. Maybe it wouldn't look so bad once it was cooked? Or maybe the Nicelys would be so busy talking they wouldn't notice anything? If Mum knew what Whiffer had done she would go bananas! And Bertie was bound to get the blame. He felt sick. Perhaps he could ask to be excused?

Angela was staring at him. "You're very quiet today," she said.

"Am I?" mumbled Bertie.

"Don't you like tomato soup? I've eaten all mine!" said Angela.

Dad collected up their bowls.

Here it comes, thought Bertie.

Mum went over to the oven and brought out the shepherd's pie.

"Oh! Good heavens!" she gasped.

Dirty Bertie

The pie looked even worse than Bertie remembered. It seemed to have suffered some sort of landslide. Gravy dripped down one side of the dish. The Nicelys stared at it boggle-eyed.

Dirty Bertie

"Goodness ... how unusual," said Mrs Nicely.

"What is it?" asked Angela.

"Shepherd's pie," said Mum, weakly. "It was fine when it went in the oven. I can't think what could have happened."

Bertie avoided her eye.

Mr Nicely laughed. "Well I'm sure it tastes delicious," he said.

I wouldn't bet on it, thought Bertie.

Mum served up the pie and passed round their plates.

Bertie held his breath. This was it — they were actually going to eat it!

The Nicelys raised their forks and chewed their food in silence. Bertie waited. No one choked or spat it out. Mrs Nicely pulled a face.

Dirty Bertie

"What an … um … interesting flavour!" she said.

"Yes, it tastes sort of nutty," said Mr Nicely.

Angela nudged Bertie. "Aren't you eating any?" she asked.

"Course I am," said Bertie. "I'm just … letting it cool down."

He breathed a sigh of relief. It was going to be okay. The shepherd's pie wouldn't win any prizes but no one suspected the truth…

Dirty Bertie

"URGH!" Mrs Nicely let out a sudden squawk.

Her husband looked up. "Oh dear, darling, are you all right?"

Mrs Nicely shook her head and pulled something out of her mouth. Bertie stared at it in horror. It was a long, white hair – exactly like the dog-hairs on the sofa.

"EWWW!" cried Suzy.

"YUCK!" cried Angela.

Mrs Nicely had gone a funny shade of green.

Mum rose to her feet. "I am SO sorry!" she said. "I don't know how it got in there. It's certainly not one of mine!"

At that moment Whiffer trotted in.

Dirty Bertie

He still had gravy stains round his mouth. Mum stared. A horrible thought crept into her mind.

The same horrible thought struck Mrs Nicely. She dropped her fork and clutched at her throat. "THE DOG!" she gasped. "I think I'm going to be SICK!"

Dirty Bertie

The Nicelys did not stay for dessert. Mrs Nicely said she would never be able to look at a shepherd's pie again. She needed to go home and lie down.

Mum tried to apologize while Dad went to fetch the Nicelys' coats.

At the front door Angela turned round. "Thank you for having me," she said politely. "But next time…"

"ANGELA!" snapped her mother. "We are going home!"

The front door slammed. Mum and Dad looked at each other.

"BERTIE!" yelled Mum.

They marched into the kitchen. But the back door was open and Bertie wasn't there. He'd just remembered something – Whiffer needed a walk and there was no time like the present.

Dirty Bertie

JACKPOT!

For Johnny and Aoife ~ D R

Thanks to Megan and Andrea for the great
story ideas ~ A M

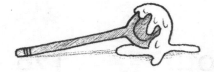

Contents

JACKPOT!

CHAPTER 1

Bertie thumped downstairs. The phone
was ringing in the hall. Maybe it was
Darren calling to say that school had
burned down! He snatched up the receiver.

"Hello?"

"Hello, is that you, Bertie?"

"Oh hi, Gran, wassup?" said Bertie.

"You sound funny," said Gran.

Dirty Bertie

"Are you eating?"

"No, jush cleaning my teef," said Bertie.

"Well, never mind that, I've got some exciting news," said Gran. "You remember we stopped off at the supermarket on Wednesday?"

"Yes?"

"And you kept on and on until I bought a lottery ticket?"

"Yes?" said Bertie.

"Well, I WON!" whooped Gran. "We won! Can you believe it?"

Bertie thought he must be dreaming but no, he was wide awake with toothpaste dribbling down his jumper.

"REALLY?" he gasped.

"Yes really!" said Gran. "I've got the ticket right here. And anyway—"

"WAHOOOOO!"

Bertie dropped the phone, leaving Gran to talk to herself. He skidded into the kitchen where Mum and Suzy were having breakfast.

"WE WON! WE WON!" he yelled.

"Won what?" said Mum.

"The lottery!" shouted Bertie.

"Oh ha, ha," jeered Suzy. "We never do the lottery."

"No, but Gran did," said Bertie. "That was her on the phone. We actually won!"

Mum and Suzy stared at Bertie as if he'd lost his mind. They waited for him to burst out laughing and admit that it was a joke. But he didn't.

Dirty Bertie

"WE'RE RICH! WE'RE RICH!" he sang, bouncing around the room.

"What's all the noise?" asked Dad, coming in. "Shouldn't you be getting ready for school, Bertie?"

"Gran just phoned," said Mum. "She's got some news…"

"WE WON THE LOTTERY!" yelled Bertie.

Dad looked at him. "You're kidding!"

Bertie had to go over it all again. It was really him they ought to thank, he explained, because he'd talked Gran into buying a ticket. In fact, when you thought about it, half the money was his.

"How much will we get?" Bertie asked.

Dad sat down heavily. "I don't know, it could be millions," he said.

Dirty Bertie

"MILLIONS!" cried Bertie.

"What *exactly* did she say to you?" asked Mum.

"Nothing, just that we won the lottery," said Bertie.

They sat round the breakfast table, trying to take it in. Bertie's mind was already going into overdrive. Millions – think of that! He'd never actually seen a million pounds. Would the postman

bring it round in his sack? Or would it come on the back of a lorry? One thing was for sure, he was definitely going to need a bigger money box!

"I could give up work," said Dad in a daze.

"We could go on our dream holiday," said Mum.

"I could have my own pony," said Suzy. "Or even two."

"Don't forget it's *my* ticket that won," Bertie reminded them.

"Gran's ticket, you mean," said Mum. "And we shouldn't get carried away. She might not want to share the money."

Bertie's face fell. Not share it? What would Gran do with a million pounds? She already got half-price travel on the bus! In any case, Gran was part of the family – she practically lived at their house! There was no way she'd keep a million pounds all to herself. He poured a second bowl of cereal.

"What are you doing?" asked Mum.

"Having breakfast," replied Bertie. "I can't go to school today, can I?"

"Too right you can," said Mum. "Now get a move on."

Bertie sighed. When he was a millionaire he definitely wasn't going to school. Spending all that money would be a full-time job. Wait till he told his friends – they would never believe it!

CHAPTER 2

Ten minutes later Bertie met Darren and
Eugene at the end of the road. Mum
had suggested they should keep their
lottery win a secret for now, but Bertie
wasn't very good at keeping secrets.
Besides, Darren and Eugene were his
best friends. He greeted them, grinning
from ear to ear.

Dirty Bertie

"You're very happy for a school day," said Darren.

"Yes, I've had a bit of good news," said Bertie. "You'll never guess what."

"You've got peanut butter sandwiches," suggested Eugene.

"You actually finished your homework," said Darren.

"Much better than that," said Bertie. "We won the lottery!"

His friends stared at him in goggle-eyed amazement.

"The lottery?" said Eugene.

"You big liar!" snorted Darren.

Bertie just went on grinning at them. This was better than the time Miss Boot's chair broke when she sat down.

"It's true," said Bertie. "But it's a secret, so don't go blabbing it around."

"You're serious?" said Darren. "How much?"

Bertie shrugged. "Dunno, probably millions."

"MILLIONS?" cried Eugene. "Woah! You'll be loaded!"

"We'll never have to walk to school again," said Darren. "We could go by helicopter!"

"I might give up school anyway," said Bertie breezily. "I can pay someone else to go for me — Know-All Nick for instance."

It wasn't a bad idea. He could hire Know-All Nick as his personal servant to carry his bag, clean his shoes and fetch important stuff — like ice cream.

Darren was thinking. "When do you get the money?" he asked.

"Pretty soon I expect," replied Bertie. "Gran's got the ticket."

Darren frowned. "Hang on, you mean it's not actually *your* ticket?" he said. "It's your gran's?"

"Well, yes," admitted Bertie. "But it was my idea, and anyway, I'm her favourite grandson."

Actually he was her *only* grandson – which was probably just as well.

£ $ ¥ € ₩

Bertie found it impossible to concentrate on lessons that morning. His attention always wandered when Miss Boot was talking, but today was worse than ever. All he could think about was one million lovely pounds. ONE MILLION! He could buy his own sweet shop,

Dirty Bertie

or a chocolate factory... He could live in
a palace with a whole room for his bug
collection...

"BERTIE!" bellowed Miss Boot. "GET
ON WITH YOUR WORK!"

"Yes, Miss." Bertie sighed. The first
thing he would do with his winnings was
buy Miss Boot a
one-way ticket to
Australia.

CHAPTER 3

Back home, Bertie slammed the front door shut and threw down his bag. His mum was in the kitchen.

"Well, did it come?" he asked eagerly.

"Did what come?" said Mum.

"The money of course! The million pounds."

"It won't come here," said Mum.

"It belongs to Gran. I've been trying to phone her all day but she's never in."

Bertie frowned. Surely Gran should be staying at home, in case the postman came.

"Anyway, I left a message," said Mum. "I said we'd take her out to celebrate tomorrow – at Dibbles' Tea Rooms."

Bertie raised his eyebrows. They never went out to tea and certainly not to Dibbles – the posh department store in town. Bertie thought that tea rooms sounded like the kind of place where people tutted when you burped. Still, there would be cakes and Gran could tell them all about their lottery win. Best of all, Dibbles had a toy department!

"Mum," said Bertie. "Can we go shopping tomorrow?"

Dirty Bertie

Mum narrowed her eyes. "I thought you hated shopping," she said.

"Only clothes shopping," said Bertie. "But I think Dibbles has a toy department."

"I'm sure it does," said Mum. "But I'll need to talk to your father."

She thought it over. Normally she avoided taking Bertie shopping like the plague. He was forever picking things up, knocking them down or complaining that he wanted to go home. But maybe just this once. After all, if it wasn't for Bertie, Gran would never have won the lottery in the first place.

£ $ ¥ € ₩

The following afternoon, Bertie's family arrived at Dibbles department store.

Dirty Bertie

"Right, Suzy and I are off to look at shoes," said Mum.

"Wait a minute, what am I supposed to do?" grumbled Dad.

"You can look after Bertie," said Mum. "He wants to go to the toy department."

"Why can't you take him?" moaned Dad.

"I'm taking Suzy," said Mum. "See you later. We're meeting Gran at three."

Dirty Bertie

Dad rolled his eyes. A whole hour in a toy department with Bertie – this was going to be torture!

Dibbles' toy department was on the fourth floor. Bertie's eyes lit up as they stepped out of the lift. It was an Aladdin's cave of wonders: board games, scooters, skateboards, super gunge shooters and gadgets galore.

Bertie picked up a pirate cutlass and swished it through the air. "AHARRRR!" he roared.

"Put that down!" hissed Dad. "You'll break something!"

"May I be of any help, sir?"

A tall, silver-haired shop assistant loomed over them.

"It's okay, thanks, we're just looking," said Dad, grabbing Bertie's sword.

"Anything special?" asked the assistant. "We have a brand new range of trampolines."

"Maybe a bit dangerous – and expensive," said Dad.

"But we're loaded!" said Bertie. "We've just won the lottery."

"Ha ha! We can all dream, can't we?" laughed the shop assistant.

"It's not a dream, it's true!" said Bertie. "We're rich!"

Suddenly they had the assistant's full attention. "Well, I *do* apologize, sir," he said. "In that case, may I show you our luxury toys over here."

Bertie gazed at the toy spaceships and gamma-ray guns. Then something else caught his eye – a gleaming red sports car, just his size.

Dirty Bertie

"Look at this, Dad!" he cried.

"Ah yes, our junior Ferrari," said the shop assistant. "It has a rechargeable battery, working headlights and a top speed of ten miles an hour."

"WOW!" said Bertie. Imagine arriving at school in his own Ferrari! Even Royston Rich hadn't got one of those.

"Can I get in?" asked Bertie, eagerly.

"By all means," said the shop assistant. Bertie climbed into the driving seat.

"How much does it cost?" asked Dad, anxiously.

The assistant showed him the price tag. Dad turned pale. It was more than he'd paid for their family car.

"VROOM! VROOM!" cried Bertie, imagining he was on the Formula One starting grid. The dashboard had lots of lights, switches and buttons. Bertie pointed to a silver key.

"What's this for?" he asked.

"Don't touch that!" cried the shop assistant.

VROOOOOOM!

The car's engine roared into life. Bertie's foot was on the accelerator and the Ferrari took off like a rocket.

"WOAH!" squawked Bertie, gripping the steering wheel. "I CAN'T STOP!"

Dirty Bertie

Customers dived out of the way as the Ferrari zoomed straight for them. Bertie turned the wheel and screeched round a corner.

"BRAKE!" yelled Dad. "USE THE BRAKE…!"

Dirty Bertie

"WHICH ONE?" wailed Bertie.
CRASH!

Too late, Bertie ploughed into a display cabinet of dolls, sending them flying in the air. Dad groaned and buried his face in his hands. He knew he should never have agreed to take Bertie shopping.

CHAPTER 4

At three o'clock, Dad and Bertie took the lift to the tea rooms. Mum and Suzy were already there, surrounded by shopping bags.

Dad rolled his eyes. "I thought you were just looking at shoes?" he said.

"We bought shoes," said Mum. "Plus one or two other things we needed.

Dirty Bertie

Anyway, how did you and Bertie get on?"

"Don't ask," sighed Dad. They'd been made to pay for all the damage Bertie had caused, which had cost a small fortune.

Dad slumped into a chair. "Let's just say it's a good job that Gran's won the lottery," he said.

"Here she comes now," said Suzy.

Dirty Bertie

Gran kissed them all and took a seat.

"This *is* a surprise," she said. "Tea at Dibbles, how nice!"

Mum smiled. "Order anything you like," she said. "It's our treat."

"Really? *Anything?*" said Bertie. He'd been eyeing the cakes and had decided to try them all.

The waiter came over. Mum ordered sandwiches, the special cake selection and champagne for the adults. She turned to Gran.

"Well!" she said. "Tell us all the details."

"How much did we win?" asked Bertie. "A million? Ten million?"

Gran blinked at them, confused. "But I explained on the phone. Didn't Bertie tell you?" she said.

"Tell us what?" said Dad.

"I won twenty pounds," said Gran.

There was a long stony silence.

"Twenty pounds?" cried Mum. "But Bertie said you'd won the lottery!"

"I won a prize, yes. I didn't win the lottery," said Gran. "I told you, Bertie, weren't you listening?"

Everyone turned to glare at Bertie.

He slid down slowly in his seat. Oops! He remembered dropping the phone and rushing off before Gran had finished speaking. It turned out they wouldn't be getting a swimming pool, servants or a Ferrari, after all.

"BERTIE!" groaned Mum.

"We should have known," said Suzy.

Dad had gone very pale. "Do you know how much today has cost us?" he said.

Just then the waiter appeared.

Dirty Bertie

"Your cakes and champagne, madam."
Bertie grabbed an iced bun and
crammed it into his mouth. He had a
feeling there might not be any more
treats for quite a while.

CHAPTER 1

Miss Boot stood at the front of class.

"Good morning, children," she said.
"As you can see, we have a visitor with
us today."

Bertie sat up. It was Mrs Nicely, his
next door neighbour! What on earth
was *she* doing in his class?

"Mrs Nicely has kindly offered to teach

a cookery class," said Miss Boot.

Mrs Nicely smiled. "Who would like to learn how to bake a cake?"

A cake? Bertie loved cakes! Mainly he liked eating them, but he was willing to have a go at making one. At home his parents didn't even let him make toast in case he burned the house down. But if he made a cake he could scoff it all himself! YUM!

"As you know, it's Mrs Fossil's last day and the staff are planning a little party for her," said Miss Boot. "What could be nicer than a special cake made by one of you?"

Bertie's face fell. No way was Mrs Fossil getting her greedy hands on *his* cake. Mrs Fossil was about a hundred years old and had been teaching at the school since the Stone Age. Today she was finally retiring. About time, too, in Bertie's opinion – he wished Miss Boot would hurry up and retire as well.

Later that morning, Bertie's class gathered in the school kitchen with Mrs Nicely.

"Now children," she said, "who can tell me what we need to make a cake?"

Amanda Fibb's hand shot up.

"Eggs," she said.

"Self-raising flour," said Know-All Nick.

"Chocolate buttons," said Bertie.

Mrs Nicely frowned. "Chocolate buttons are not essential."

"They are if it's a chocolate button cake," argued Bertie.

Mrs Nicely silently counted to ten. When she'd agreed to teach a cookery class, no one had warned her it would be with Bertie's class. The boy was a walking nightmare and his manners were appalling.

"Please leave your nose alone, Bertie," she sighed. "Now, we are going to make a simple sponge cake. Once it's baked, you can decorate it any way you like."

Bertie eyed the jars of cake decorations greedily. There were sprinkles, stars, silver balls, chocolate buttons and chocolate shavings. His cake would definitely need all of them.

Mrs Nicely showed them how to make a cake mix by weighing out the ingredients. Then she put them into pairs to have a go. Luckily Bertie got paired with Darren. He read the recipe.

"What's 300g of sugar?" Bertie asked.

"Don't ask me," said Darren. "Don't we have to weigh it?"

"That'll take forever," said Bertie. "It's quicker to just tip it all in."

He poured in the whole jar and added the butter. Next came the flour and the eggs.

Darren inspected the sloppy yellow mixture.

"Is it meant to have bits of eggshell?" he asked.

Bertie sighed — some people were so fussy! He tried to fish out the bits with his fingers but they were too slippery. What did it matter? A few bits of eggshell would add a nice crunch.

Dirty Bertie

"What's next?" Bertie asked.

"Beat well until mixed," Darren read out. Bertie grabbed the wooden spoon and attacked the bowl.

THWACK! BASH! SPLAT!

"Not so hard, Bertie!" cried Mrs Nicely. "You're slopping it everywhere!"

"Sorry," mumbled Bertie. "Darren said to beat it up."

Once it was done, Darren poured the mixture into a cake tin, ready for the oven. He checked the recipe.

"Hang on," he said. "We missed out the pinch of salt." He reached for the salt jar but found it empty. "Where's it all gone?" he asked.

"That's not salt, it's sugar," said Bertie.

"No, it's not, you dummy! Look at the label!" cried Darren.

Bertie's mouth fell open. He had put a ton of salt in their cake mix!

"The recipe says a pinch, not the whole jar!" said Darren.

Bertie shrugged. How was he meant to know? Sugar and salt looked exactly the same.

"Calm down, it'll be all right," he said.

"All right?" moaned Darren. "Cakes are meant to be sweet. Ours will taste like a bag of crisps!"

CHAPTER 2

Bertie and Darren inspected their sponge cake, which was cooling off after baking.

"Looks okay to me," said Bertie, poking it with a finger.

Darren pulled a face. "Well I'm not eating it," he said. "It'll taste of salt."

"Once we decorate it who's going to know?" asked Bertie.

"Anyone who tastes it," replied Darren.

"But they won't," said Bertie. "It's *our* cake and no one's going to touch it. At least they won't want it for Mrs Fossil's party."

Mrs Nicely clapped her hands for silence.

"Right, children, now for my favourite part," she said. "You can ice your cake with any flavour you like and then add the decorations. Remember, I will be judging the cakes and the best one will be presented to Mrs Fossil."

Bertie snorted. Luckily their cake didn't stand a chance. On the next table, Know-All Nick and Amanda Fibb were decorating a perfect golden sponge. It had lemon icing and tiny sugar flowers. *Trust smarty pants Nick to show off,* thought Bertie.

They set to work decorating their
own cake. Darren slopped on thick,
gloopy brown icing. Next they added
chocolate sprinkles, chocolate buttons,
chocolate stars and chocolate shavings.

"There!" said Bertie. "I think it looks
pretty good."

"You haven't tasted it," said Darren
glumly.

Dirty Bertie

The cakes were laid out on a long table for Mrs Nicely to judge. She moved down the line until she reached a brown mud pie, buried under a gloopy mountain of chocolate.

"Good heavens! Who made this one?" she gasped.

Dirty Bertie

Bertie raised his hand. "Me and Darren."

"I might have known," sighed Mrs Nicely. "Well, it's very, er ... big."

She hurried on to the other cakes.

Dirty Bertie

"I must say that *some* of these cakes look delicious," she said. "But one stands out from the rest. Who made this luscious lemon cake?"

Amanda Fibb and Know-All Nick stepped forward, beaming proudly.

"Wonderful!" said Mrs Nicely. "Perfectly baked and I love the little sugar flowers. Mrs Fossil will be delighted."

Dirty Bertie

HUH! thought Bertie. Who wanted to eat Nick's drippy old lemon cake? It didn't even have any chocolate! Mrs Fossil was welcome to it.

The bell rang for break time.

"Now, children, always leave the kitchen tidy," said Mrs Nicely. "Bertie and Darren, you can stay behind to clear the tables."

Bertie rolled his eyes. Why did he always get picked for the rotten jobs?

"Can't we go now?" grumbled Bertie after five minutes. "We're missing break."

"One more thing," said Mrs Nicely. "Move all these cakes on to the side so they can be collected at home time."

She hurried off to the staff room.

"What about our cake?" said Bertie.

"You take it home, I don't want it," said Darren.

"I bet Whiffer will eat it, he eats anything," sighed Bertie. It seemed a terrible waste.

The cake was dripping chocolate on to the worktop.

Bertie frowned. "It's starting to melt."

"Stick it in the fridge," suggested Darren, "or we'll have to wipe the tables again."

Bertie opened the fridge, which was packed full. On the top shelf sat Nick's luscious lemon cake that Mrs Nicely had set aside for the party. Bertie took it out, and replaced it with their chocolate blob cake.

"What are you doing?" asked Darren.

"Making room for ours," said Bertie.

Dirty Bertie

"But that's Nick's cake for the party!"

"So?" said Bertie. "It can go over there with the— Ooops!"

He accidentally tilted the plate and the cake slid off, hitting the floor.

SPLAT!

Bertie and Darren stared in horror.

"Now look what you've done!" cried
Darren.

Bertie tried to scrape the lemon cake
back on to the plate. It didn't look quite
as luscious as before. The sugar flowers
were smashed and half of the icing
remained stuck to the floor.

"What are we going to do?" groaned
Bertie.

"Don't ask me, *you* dropped it!" said
Darren.

Bertie looked around in a panic. Mrs
Nicely would go bonkers. He opened
the nearest cupboard and hid the lemon
cake behind some saucepans.

"Come on!" he said. "Let's get out of
here!"

CHAPTER 3

Back in class, Bertie and Darren didn't
mention their little accident. They
didn't even tell Eugene in case anyone
overheard. Mrs Fossil's farewell party
was taking place in the staff room at
lunchtime. Bertie pictured the moment
when they came to present the cake and
found it gone. At least no one could pin

the blame on him.

DRRRRING! The lunch bell rang. The class hurried out, but Bertie and his friends weren't fast enough.

"Bertie, Darren!" boomed Miss Boot. "I have a little job for you. And you, too, Eugene."

"But Miss, it's lunchtime!" moaned Bertie.

"This won't take long," said Miss Boot. "I need two children to serve sandwiches at the party."

Normally she would have chosen two sensible children but they'd all run off.

Bertie groaned. "Do we *have* to?"

"Splendid, I knew I could rely on you," said Miss Boot. "Run down to the staff room and I'll join you in a minute. Not you, Eugene."

Bertie and Darren trailed off. This was turning into one of those days.

"Now, Eugene," said Miss Boot. "I want you to fetch the party cake from the fridge in the kitchen. It's a surprise, so don't let Mrs Fossil see it."

Eugene nodded. At least he didn't have to stand around serving food like a waiter. He hurried off to the kitchen. The fridge stood in the corner. On the top shelf he found a cake – but not the one he was expecting. Hadn't

Dirty Bertie

Mrs Nicely picked Nick's luscious lemon cake for the party? Eugene asked a dinner lady.

"'Scuse me… Miss Boot sent me to fetch a cake?" he said.

"That's right, it's in the fridge," said the dinner lady.

"You mean this one?"

"Must be, if it's in there," said the dinner lady.

Eugene shrugged. Miss Boot must know what she was doing – although the cake looked exactly like Bertie and Darren's chocolate blob cake.

Five minutes later Eugene knocked at the staff room door.

Miss Skinner, the Head, answered. "Yes?"

"I brought the cake," said Eugene.

Miss Skinner stared. "Is that it? Good grief! You'd better put it on the table."

Eugene set the cake down where he was told. He hoped Mrs Fossil liked chocolate, because there was plenty of it.

CHAPTER 4

Bertie glanced at the clock – he was starving! Mrs Nicely was watching him like a hawk while she made the tea. So far, all he'd managed to steal was one measly cucumber sandwich from the plate. How long did they have to stand here? Mrs Fossil's party was as dull as a Monday morning. There were no games, sweets or prizes — just teachers standing around yakking and drinking tea.

Darren appeared at Bertie's side.

"We're done for," he muttered. "I've just seen the cake they're giving her."

"So?" said Bertie.

"It's *our* chocolate cake!" said Darren.

Bertie gaped. "What? It can't be!"

"IT IS!" said Darren. "See for yourself. They must have got the wrong one."

"But I left our cake in the fridge," said Bertie.

"Exactly," said Darren. "That's where the party cake was until you dropped it!"

Bertie turned pale. This was a disaster! He'd hoped they'd choose another cake to replace Nick's lemon cake, but not *theirs*. Anything but that.

"It's got salt in it!" hissed Bertie.

"You're telling me – a whole jar!" said Darren. "They'll be sick as dogs!"

Bertie was starting to feel a bit sick himself.

"Where is it? We've got to do something!" he whispered.

Darren pointed to the table across the room. Bertie pushed his way through the crowd towards it. But just then Miss Skinner clapped her hands…

"Thank you all for coming," she said. "I just want to say how much we're all going to miss dear Mrs Fossil. She has taught at this school for twenty-five years…"

Bertie reached the table. If he could just hide the chocolate cake they were saved.

Dirty Bertie

"…And so," said Miss Skinner,
"we'd like to present you with a little
something the children have made.
Bertie, would you bring the cake,
please?"

Bertie gulped. "M-me?"

"Yes, hurry up."

Bertie turned pale. Everyone in the room was waiting for him! There was no escape. He carried the cake over to Miss Skinner as if it was a ticking time-bomb. Mrs Fossil's face fell when she saw the blobby mess on the plate.

"Oh," she said. "It's very … um … brown, isn't it?"

"Yes, but I'm sure it tastes delicious," said Miss Skinner. "Let me cut everyone a piece."

Bertie watched in horror as Miss Skinner cut thick slices of cake and handed them round to all the teachers.

Darren edged towards the door. Bertie stood frozen to the spot as Mrs Fossil bit into her slice of cake. She chewed for a moment. Her face turned purple. She clutched at her throat.

"URRRGH!" she croaked. "WATER!"

"I beg your pardon?" said Miss Skinner.

"It's SALTY!" gasped Mrs Fossil. "Are you trying to *poison* me?"

Around the room, teachers were gulping and gasping and looking as if they might  be sick on their plates.

Miss Skinner tried the cake and immediately spat it out.

"*Eugh!* What *is* this?" she cried. "Mrs Nicely, which child made this cake?"

Mrs Nicely had gone red. "But this is the wrong cake!" she said. "It's not the one I chose at all. This is *Bertie's* chocolate cake!"

"BERTIE?" boomed Miss Boot.

"BERTIE!" roared Miss Skinner.

They both turned in time to see Bertie trying to sneak out of the door.

Miss Boot beckoned him over with a long finger.

"BERTIE! Come here!" she smiled. "I've got a lovely chocolate cake that needs finishing…"

DEMON DOLLY

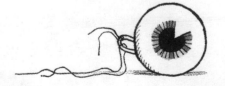

CHAPTER 1

Bertie thumped upstairs. He was playing Hide and Seek. Darren was also hiding while Eugene was 'it'.

Where to hide? The bathroom? His bedroom? Wait, Suzy's room, of course! That was the last place Eugene would look. Bertie sneaked in, closing the door.

"Coming, ready or not!" yelled Eugene.

Dirty Bertie

Quick, under the bed, thought Bertie. He dashed over…

CRUNCH!

Bertie looked down. Yikes! He'd trodden on Molly Dolly!

Suzy had had Molly Dolly since she was four. She was her favourite doll – the only one Suzy refused to part with. Bertie picked her up. Her head lolled to one side then fell off. No!

Bertie tried to jam it back on. One of the blue eyes popped out and rolled under the bed.

Help! Suzy would go bananas when she found out. Bertie wasn't allowed in her room on pain

Dirty Bertie

of death. He wrestled with the doll's
head, but it was hopeless. He'd really
done it this time.

BLAM! The door burst open.

"FOUND YOU!" cried Eugene
triumphantly. "I got Darren, too."

"Only because I sneezed," said
Darren, trailing in. "What's that?"

Bertie held up the headless doll.
"It's Suzy's. I sort of trod on
it," he groaned.

Darren shrugged. "So what? It's only a stupid doll."

"Not to Suzy," said Bertie. "It's Molly Dolly. Gran gave it to her and she goes mad if anyone even touches it."

"She's lost her head," Eugene pointed out.

"I know that," sighed Bertie. "And I can't get it back on."

They took it in turns to try and fix Molly's head. Darren bashed it with his fist, but that didn't work either. Bertie sank down on the bed in despair.

"Glue," said Eugene. "Where do you keep the glue?"

They found some glue in the kitchen and set to work. Pretty soon most of the glue was on Molly's face and hair. But it hadn't helped. Molly's head was

stuck on, but it lolled
to one side. With
one eye missing,
she looked like
something out of a
horror film.

Darren grinned.
"If you ask me it's
a big improvement,"
he said.

"It's not funny!" moaned Bertie.

Suzy would guess who'd done it
right away. Her scream would be heard
halfway down the road. She'd tell Mum
and Dad, and they'd make him pay for
a new doll out of his pocket money.
Unless… Bertie suddenly saw a way out.
It was tough on Molly, but she *was* only
a doll…

"We've got to get rid of her," he said. "If Suzy can't find Molly, she won't know what happened."

"She'll blame you anyway," Darren argued.

"Maybe, but she won't be able to prove anything," said Bertie. "I'll say I never touched her doll."

He looked around for somewhere to hide Molly. Suzy was at Bella's house, but she'd be back soon. He had to act fast. The minute Suzy noticed Molly was missing she'd search every room in the house. Bertie broke into a smile. Molly wouldn't *be* in the house – she'd be somewhere no one would find her. He hurried downstairs and went outside to the dustbins. Opening the brown bin, he dangled Molly by one leg.

"Ah! Poor thing!" sighed Eugene.

PLOP! Bertie dropped Molly into
the rubbish, pushing her down under
the soggy layers of potato peel and tea
bags.

"Bye-bye, Molly," he said, closing the
lid. "Don't lose your head!"

CHAPTER 2

"Do-do-doo, do-do-doo!"

Bertie always sang to himself when cleaning his teeth before bedtime. Mainly because he knew it drove his sister mad.

Suzy poked her head round the door. "Have you been in my room?" she demanded.

Bertie stopped singing.

Dirty Bertie

"WHAT?" he said.

"My room – have you been nosing around?" repeated Suzy.

"Why would I go in your stinky old room?" asked Bertie.

"I can't find Molly Dolly," said Suzy. "She was there when I went to school."

Bertie gulped, swallowing a mouthful of toothpaste. He'd forgotten about the doll. Still, he was safe – he'd disposed of the evidence.

"*Well*, have you seen her?" asked Suzy, glaring.

"Seen who?"

"Molly Dolly!" snapped Suzy.

"No!" said Bertie. "I haven't touched your dopey doll."

"Well, someone has. Did one of your smelly friends go in my room?" said Suzy.

Dirty Bertie

"No! I told you!" cried Bertie.

"Hmm." Suzy narrowed her eyes. "If you're lying, you are in *big* trouble," she warned.

Bertie leaned against the wall and breathed a sigh of relief. He'd got away with it. Suzy couldn't prove a thing. In a couple of days the bin men would collect the rubbish and Molly Dolly would be history.

Back in her bedroom, Suzy searched her room again. She could have sworn that Molly was there earlier. Maybe she'd fallen under the bed? She got down on her hands and knees to look. No Molly – but something small and shiny caught her eye. She reached a

hand under the bed. A tiny blue glass
eye stared back at her.

Molly Dolly had blue eyes! Suzy
frowned. Someone had been in here and
no prizes for guessing who – her bogey-
nosed little brother. But if this was Molly's
eye, where was the rest of her?

Suzy had a terrible thought. She
rushed downstairs and hurried outside.
She opened the brown bin.

"NOOOO!"

Poor Molly Dolly lay buried under
tea bags and potato peel. As Suzy

picked her up, Molly's head came off in
her hand. Her face was sticky and she
squinted from one eye.

"You wait, Bertie!" said Suzy. She'd
pay him back for this. She'd put a worm
in his lunch box; she'd leave a slug
in his bed… But would that bother
Bertie? No! He loved worms, slugs and
disgusting things!

Suzy stroked Molly's sticky hair. Hang
on… Bertie thought the doll was gone
forever – well, he was in for a shock.
Molly Dolly was
about to rise
from the dead!

CHAPTER 3

It was almost midnight. Bertie lay in bed, fast asleep.

BOO-HOO-HOO!

His eyes blinked open. What was that? Had he been dreaming? He was sure that he heard crying.

BOO-HOO-HOO!

There it was again – a faint sobbing

coming from somewhere outside his room. Maybe Whiffer had escaped from the kitchen and got upstairs? But it didn't sound like Whiffer. He'd be scratching at the door and whining to be let in, or jumping on the bed. Bertie sat up and listened.

"WUH-HUH-HUH!"

It sounded like a baby crying! The hairs prickled on the back of Bertie's neck. There were no babies in the house, were there? When his parents had tried to sell the house Bertie had told visitors that it was haunted. But surely he'd made that up...

CREEEEEAK!

What was that? Bertie pulled the duvet higher. There was something out on the landing!

Dirty Bertie

"H-hello?" he croaked. "Who's there?"
Silence.

Suddenly a face rose into view: a tiny,
pale face with wild hair and one staring
eye...

"BERTIE!" the doll hissed. "It's me!"
"ARRRRRGH!"

Dirty Bertie

Bertie dived under his covers and lay there breathing hard. No, it wasn't possible! Molly Dolly was gone and buried in the dustbin. Besides, she was a doll – she couldn't move or speak … not unless she was … A GHOST!

Bertie shivered. He peeped his head slowly above the duvet. Phew – it had gone! He flopped back on his pillow, his heart beating fast. This was his own fault. He'd dumped poor Molly in the dustbin. Now her ghost had returned to haunt him!

Back in her room, Suzy smiled to herself. Her plan had worked like a dream. With a little sticky tape she'd managed to attach Molly's head back

on. Bertie had practically jumped out
of his skin when the doll rose up and
spoke like a ghost. She wished she
could have seen his terrified face. But
she wasn't finished yet – the haunting
had only just begun. Suzy tied Molly to a
stick and carefully poked her out of the
window. Bertie's bedroom was just next
door.

Bertie tossed and turned, trying to get
to sleep. *There are no ghosts,* he told
himself. It was just his imagination playing
tricks. In the morning he'd laugh about
this – fancy thinking that a ghost dolly
was haunting him! Ha ha! It was the
most stupid idea in—

TAP, TAP, TAP!

Dirty Bertie

Hold on, what was that noise?

TAP, TAP, TAP!

Something was tapping at his window. Bertie kept his eyes shut tight, too scared to look. It was no use, he had to see what it was. Slowly he turned his head and peeped…

ARRGH! There it was at the window! The same staring face with one eye. Molly Dolly was trying to get in!

Dirty Bertie

"WAAAAH!"

Bertie dived out of bed and bolted along to his parents' room.

"HELP! SAVE ME!" he gasped, barging in.

Dad moaned. Mum sat up in bed.

"Bertie, what on earth's the matter?" she said.

"IT'S AFTER ME!" wailed Bertie. "DON'T LET IT GET ME!"

"What is? What are you talking about?" said Mum.

"MOLLY DOLLY!" cried Bertie. "She's a … a ghost!"

Mum rubbed her eyes wearily.

"It's one o'clock in the morning," she groaned. "You just had a nightmare."

"I didn't!" cried Bertie. "It was at the window – I saw it!"

Dirty Bertie

Mum got out of bed and threw on her dressing gown. She took Bertie back to his room.

"Where? Where's this ghost?" she demanded.

"It was right there – at the window. I saw it!" answered Bertie.

Mum rolled her eyes. "There's nothing there!" she said. "You just had a bad dream. Now *please* can we all get some sleep?"

CHAPTER 4

Bertie stared at his alarm clock. It was a quarter to two. He wished morning would come. Every time he closed his eyes, the wind moaned or a floorboard creaked and he thought it was the ghost. If he ever survived this, he swore he'd never set foot in Suzy's bedroom again. Maybe Molly Dolly would leave him alone if he promised to be good?

In the next bedroom, Suzy had one last
trick to play – something that would
scare the pants off her horrible little
brother. She rummaged through her
cupboard until she found what she
wanted – Kutie Kitty. It was years since
she'd played with the toy kitten. She
hoped that the battery still worked.

Dirty Bertie

Bertie's eyes snapped open. What was that? *Keep calm, it's only the wind,* he told himself. He should have shut the door when he came back to bed. Perhaps he should get up now and close it…

WHIRR! CLICK, CLICK!

Bertie's blood ran cold. Nooo! It was back. The one-eyed ghost. It was out on the landing. If he got out of bed maybe he could slam the door in its face. But that wouldn't work – ghosts could walk *through* doors!

WHIRR! CLICK, CLICK!

Bertie shrank down under his covers. *Please, please, don't let it get me!* he prayed.

Suddenly a strange creature appeared

in the doorway. Argh! There it was! The ghost of Molly – and it was walking! It had grown four legs and a furry white body!

WHIRR! CLICK, CLICK! WHIRR!

The ghost doll plodded closer, twitching its head.

Dirty Bertie

"ARRRRRRGHHHH!"

Bertie's yell was loud enough to wake the whole house. He shot out of bed, leaped over the doll and scrambled out of the door.

Seconds later, he dived on to his parents' bed.

"MU-UUM! HEEELP!"

"BERTIE!" groaned Mum.

"Not again," moaned Dad.

"IT'S AFTER ME!" babbled Bertie. "Don't let it get me."

"Bertie, how many times…? There's nothing there," said Mum.

"There is! It's got four furry legs and one eye," wailed Bertie.

Mum jumped out of bed. She couldn't take much more of this. She dragged Bertie back to his room and snapped on the light.

"LOOK!" she cried. "THERE IS
NOTHING THERE!"

Something lay on the floor, whirring
and kicking its legs. Bertie bent down
and picked it up. It was a toy kitten –
with Molly's head.

Bertie stared in disbelief.

"*This* is what you were scared of?"
cried Mum.

Bertie sheepishly nodded his head.
This was Suzy's doing. She must have
found Molly buried in the bin and
planned her revenge. Worse still, he
couldn't tell on her without landing
himself in big trouble.

Mum was frowning. "Hang on,"
she said. "Isn't this Molly Dolly? What
happened to her head?"

Dirty Bertie

Bertie turned red. "Um … is it really that late?" he said, looking at the clock. "I'd better get to bed, I've got school in the morning."

Mum gave him a withering look and stormed back to her room.

Bertie switched off the light and climbed into bed. Peace at last. No more babies crying or ghosts at the window. But wait, what was this on his pillow? Something small and shiny. He switched on his bedside lamp.

YARGGGHHHH! IT WAS SOMEBODY'S EYEBALL!

Out now: